DEAD
POPULAR

SUE WALLMAN

Scholastic Children's Books
An imprint of Scholastic Ltd
Euston House, 24 Eversholt Street, London, NW1 1DB, UK
Registered office: Westfield Road, Southam, Warwickshire, CV47 0RA
SCHOLASTIC and associated logos are trademarks and/or
registered trademarks of Scholastic Inc.

First published in the UK by Scholastic Ltd, 2019

Text copyright © Sue Wallman, 2019

The right of Sue Wallman to be identified as the
author of this work has been asserted.

ISBN 978 1407 19294 9

Printed by CPI Group (UK) Ltd, Croydon, CR0 4YY
Papers used by Scholastic Children's Books are made
from wood grown in sustainable forests.

1 3 5 7 9 10 8 6 4 2

This is a work of fiction. Names, characters, places, incidents
and dialogues are products of the author's imagination or are used
fictitiously. Any resemblance to actual people, living or dead,
events or locales is entirely coincidental.

www.scholastic.co.uk

With thanks to my brother, Nick Franklin

THE BEACH

The waves rolled on to the sand with a slow, gentle swish. It was the loudest sound on the beach. From somewhere up on the cliffs, beyond the wind-stunted trees, came the distant thump of music and the hum of excited chatter. Light from the partial moon gave the water a slight shine, like tarnished metal. Small crabs the size of coins burrowed in the damp sand and insects skittered on the surface. Seaweed lay in stranded heaps.

Beyond the narrow strip of sand were pebbles, smooth, pockmarked and occasionally sharp. In the half-light it was hard to see what was pebble and what was shadow. At the bottom of the cliffs were rocks and tufty bits of grass, and sun-bleached litter, which had been deposited by the wind, and trapped. The air was warm and the sea breeze was slight.

A perfect autumn day had slipped into a mild night.

In daylight hours, children had clambered on the rocks, seeing how far they could go before having to jump back down on to the pebbles.

Tonight, a teenage girl in a stunning black dress was sprawled inelegantly across three large rocks. Face down, bones shattered, blood seeping out of her lifeless body.

CHAPTER 1

I stared at myself in the mirror above the chest of drawers. I was Kate Lynette Jordan-Ferreira, future award-winning sculptor, not-bad singer, thrower of an unexpectedly successful beach party in the third form, and brand new House Prefect. And, it had to be said, someone who turned heads. I was beautiful. It was a fact, and part of who I was. This was my room, the coolest one in Pankhurst House, the most sought-after of the three boarding houses for girls at Mount Norton School. Some notable girls had passed through Pankhurst throughout the years and we were proud to be following in their footsteps.

Lifting the edge of the duvet cover towards me, I observed with satisfaction the pale peach-coloured piping.

1

Only fifth-formers were entitled to that colour in their rooms. It matched the curtains. Lower years had to put up with the vulgarity of garish orange. *Ohmygod Orange*, Meribel called it.

Where *were* Meribel and Lo? I sat up. We'd agreed to arrive early and soak in the top-floor experience before we had to join in the bustle of the new term. The announcement that I'd been made House Prefect happened at the end of the summer term, and I'd been entitled to choose who would join me in these much-coveted rooms as my deputies. Nobody was in any doubt I'd choose those two. Every successful person at Mount Norton had at least two best friends in their boarding house they could name as deputies if called upon. I'd picked up on that early on.

I hoped I'd earned the House Prefect title, but I knew it might have been secured by my father in return for a hefty donation to the school, and the overgenerous gifts we sent to the housemistress Miss Wibberton, also known as Wibbz, at the end of every term. Being considered for the role wasn't a transparent process but, to be honest, I didn't much care if the role wasn't exactly earned.

Unfortunately Wibbz had been sacked in the holidays; word on the group chats was she'd shown some prospective parents round while drunk. We were shocked she'd been booted out, but not so much about the alcohol. The Majestic Wine delivery-van driver and Wibbz were well acquainted, and had been for years. There was a new temporary housemistress whom I was yet to meet, as she'd been talking to the newbie first-formers in the junior common room when I'd arrived. She'd sounded young and stern, the complete opposite of the Wibbster.

I willed my friends to come through the door, so we could get on with being *us*. This year mattered. It might be the last for which the three of us were together. If Lo didn't get another scholarship, she'd have to go to sixth form somewhere else. If Meribel carried on not doing any work and going on modelling assignments, she might be slung out too.

Bouncing off the bed, I went across to the large sash window. Nobody could say that view wasn't spectacular. Beyond the black metal fire escape and brick-paved courtyard, the back lane and the squat, expensive bungalows with more glass than brick, was the sea. Today it was glorious and glittering. Further up the lane, out of sight of my window, were the large car park and the start of two paths, a zigzag one which led down to the beach, and the other which went along the cliffs until it eventually hit a hotel. Walkers and runners were funnelled round it and through an executive housing estate to reach the next part of the coastal path.

A couple of seagulls screeched, and then it was silent again. The large window unlocked easily and opened upwards smoothly. Before I could step out on to the fire escape, there was a noise from the landing and I rushed to my door.

"Ta-dah," I said as I pulled my door open dramatically.

3

"Welcome!" There was nobody there. The building was old and creaky, and thinking somebody was there when they weren't had happened before, when I had a room on the first and then second floor. It was unnerving, but for some reason the sharp loneliness of it almost winded me. I thought of Elsie Gran, my grandmother, driving home without me and my substantial luggage.

I moved to the top of the stairs and sat down, planting my bare toes in the woven squares of tough carpet. I'd spent a lot of my life sitting on various stairs, waiting or listening.

"Kate?" Meribel's voice sung up the stairwell. I'd signed in. She knew I was here.

I sprang to my feet and peered over the banister to see her black hair, sleeked into a ponytail, brown toned arms and a turquoise crop top.

"Woo-hoo!" I shouted.

She tipped her head back so she could see me and shrieked, "Yay! I can't believe we're the top-floor squad."

Her bracelets rattled as she charged up the remaining stairs, clutching her jacket, which she discarded on the top banister. She hugged me lightly as she air-kissed me, stooping to be approximately near my cheeks. "I'm so jealous Lo got to spend time with you over the summer and I didn't."

"Next time," I said.

"It's been so busy. Work, boyfriend ... life." She flopped her head to mime exhaustion, and then righted it

4

to say, "Let's see these rooms, then."

I hadn't done more than glance into the other two rooms, but now I showed Meribel round like a proud estate agent. The only flaw was the cracked tile in Meribel's shower, and once we'd established it wasn't a hair, she stopped freaking out.

Next September we'd be across the road in a purpose-built sixth-form block called Davison. Its ugliness was offset by the fact that it had an enormous common room, open to either sex from any boarding house, and as fifth-formers we were now entitled to use it.

This year we'd have the best of both worlds: the third floor to ourselves and access to Davison common room. It was going to be fun.

Meribel, Lo and I had seen our rooms when they'd belonged to last year's fifth-formers. It was an offence to walk into someone else's room without permission, but the then House Prefect, Veronica, and her two deputies were on a theatre trip to London and there'd been no staff around to catch us.

My room had been Veronica's; I'd been astounded by it, and not just because of the view and the all-important fire escape. There'd been an eye-blast of colourful, textured canvases of varying sizes, but one so large it covered almost the entire wall. I'd wondered how she'd got it into the room, until on closer examination I saw that it had been pieced together in six separate parts. Bottles of paint stood amongst her make-up. Piles of *Vogue, Harpers Bazaar,*

Porter and *Elle* were stacked in one corner, and there was a compact sewing machine on top of her dark-wood desk. She must have had the desk delivered; it wasn't standard issue. I didn't remember much about how the other rooms were decorated. I suppose I knew from the beginning I wanted that one.

"This is fabulous," said Meribel as we walked around. "But there should be a lift up here. Three staircases to get to my room is a killer."

"Go over to Davison and speak to Veronica," I joked. Veronica liked starting petitions, but usually about more noble things.

"Hi!"

We wheeled round. Lo always seemed smaller in real life than she did in my mind. Her coppery hair was loose and wavy. She only ever tied it back for exams, dancing or smart occasions. It gave the impression she was more relaxed than she was. Her skin had freckled over the summer, making her eyes appear even bluer. She accidentally gave off strong English upper-class vibes – before she opened her mouth and spoke with her Essex accent.

"Lois!" I squealed. "Finally!"

I rushed to hug her. The last time I'd seen her was at Pisa airport, after she'd spent a week with me and my parents at their three-month rental.

"You OK?" I asked.

Lo grimaced. "Yeah, apart from a train journey in a

carriage with the world's loudest, most annoying kids in the seats behind me."

I nodded sympathetically. Meribel and I were always driven to school: Meribel by her family's chauffeur, me by Elsie Gran in her old Volvo, listening to audiobook thrillers.

Lo hugged Meribel, and we hustled Lo into her room, where she stared round it as if she couldn't remember any of the details from when we'd done our reconnaissance.

"This room is huge. It's worth being friends with you, Kate Jordan-Ferreira," she said, with raised eyebrows. I knew she meant it playfully.

"Time for a catch up," I announced and plummeted on to her bed. The others piled on and we arranged the pillows around us with me in the middle. It was strange to think that before I'd joined the school in the third form the two of them hadn't really been friends. We'd got to know each other on a school-organized trip to a gig in Ryemouth, and the three of us had sung and laughed all the way back on the minibus.

Meribel was the one with the height and desire to pursue modelling, but all three of us were striking. We made a powerful threesome.

Meribel told us about her autumn-wear shoot in Berlin, sweating in jumpers and coats in a humid park. Lo described arriving at a muddy field for a camping trip with her family, including her younger brother and an unfeasibly large number of cousins. She hilariously re-

7

enacted the arguments about where they were going to pitch their tents, switching accents seamlessly. I showed them a video on my phone of me singing at my father's birthday party in a bar in Milan. I belted out the top notes like a pro. The singing lessons at school had really helped, and so had the figure-hugging dress I'd bought for the occasion. The best thing about the video was the way my father looked at me with a pinch of pride. Meribel and Lo whooped more loudly than anybody had in the bar.

"What's Wibbz's replacement like?" I asked, as I frisbeed my phone to the end of the bed, out of sight, so I wouldn't obsess over the fact that Elsie Gran hadn't messaged to say she'd got back home in one piece. She often forgot. It was fine.

Meribel, who had just placed her head on my shoulder, lifted it. "You mean you managed to avoid her? Lucky you. She shook my hand and practically crushed my fingers, and gave me an intense stare."

"Me too," said Lo. "Her name is Ms Calding. She's about one hundred years younger than Wibbz and not so wobbly."

"Yeah, she's pinched and bony, but not in a camera-loving way," said Meribel.

"The first-formers will be petrified of her," said Lo. "Perhaps that's the point. At least she's temporary."

"Anyone's going to be a disappointment after Wibbz," I said.

We took a moment to reminisce about some of Wibbz's finer moments, such as the time she dropped the engraved glass Pankhurst Achiever's Award in assembly, and when she sat down too heavily on a chair in the junior common room and it collapsed, taking several of us to heave her out of its frame. The time she went shopping and left her new underwear in the junior common room. It had been fascinatingly enormous and surprisingly frilly, and she'd taken it well when she discovered it dangling from the top corners of an oil painting in the dining hall.

"So ... mini announcement," said Lo when there was a pause. "I have to work hard this year. Less time-wasting at the beach for me."

"Time at the beach is never wasted," said Meribel. "Sea air is good for your skin. Fact." She patted her cheek.

"There'll be a record number of applications for the sixth-form scholarships," said Lo.

"Since when did this start being a school parents fought to get their kids into?" said Meribel. "I thought the mission statement was to be good at the arts but a little bit crap on the academic side."

"It probably got bigged up in a newspaper supplement," I said.

That prompted Meribel to tell us about an article she'd read about a café in Spain where they simulated earthquakes. She started searching on her phone for it. I closed my eyes. You could always hear the sea in Pankhurst, so long as a window was open. It was good to be back.

9

"It feels weird being here again, don't you think?" asked Lo, half-reading my mind.

"A bit," I said. I was used to switching between places, having had lots of practice. I'd bounced between various schools: Dubai where my parents lived, whichever Mediterranean spot they chose to rent over the summer to get away from the desert heat, and Elsie Gran's little house crammed with broken furniture and things lying around waiting to be recycled.

"Feels the same as ever," said Meribel. She yawned and stretched, and I tickled her armpit. She shrieked and tried to lift my arm to retaliate.

The bell rang and we flopped down on the bed, and lay there with Lo.

"My stomach's rumbling," said Meribel. "D'you think Squirrel's made any of those no-bake date-and-cranberry brownies today?"

"Or proper brownies," said Lo. "With actual chocolate in. Or her mini cupcakes with exploded blueberries."

It wasn't cool to go down immediately after the bell rang, even if we knew in this case it meant tea and cake in the junior common room. We waited a while before rolling off the bed, checking our faces on our phones, and strolling down the three sets of stairs.

Meribel was first, and I bumped into her at the bottom because she'd stopped abruptly. I saw a woman ahead of us, with dark blonde hair in a blunt bob standing with her thin arms crossed. She was maybe early twenties, pale-skinned with no make-up and dressed in a three-quarter-sleeved stiff white shirt tucked into tailored navy trousers. In the context of Mount Norton staff she was relatively attractive, but that really wasn't saying much. I knew she must be Ms Calding.

The three of us spread out into a line.

"Girls," she said as she approached us, her voice matching the crispness of that shirt. "Lateness won't be tolerated. You are to come downstairs immediately after the bell goes." She looked at my skirt, many inches above the limit. "Own clothes must conform to regulations." And then she thrust her hand forward for me to shake, and said, "Kate Jordan-Ferreira, we haven't yet met. You're House Prefect, I gather? I'm sure we'll get to know each other well." Her handshake was cold and firm, and her smile wasn't reflected in her eyes. I wondered if she knew what a big deal it was being House Prefect. I would be asked to contribute my views on anything to do with Pankhurst. I would be giving speeches throughout the year, and sitting in on interviews with potential new girls. I had the power to give behaviour points to girls in the lower years, and I could skip meal queues, and reserve whichever table I wanted in the dining hall.

I had a suspicion life at Pankhurst was about to change, and not for the better.

CHAPTER 2

"Oh, God, another year of Clemmie," said Meribel as we walked into the junior common room for first-day tea.

We knew where Clemmie would be – on the velvet sofa next to Paige, with her other admirers close by. She looked exactly the same as she had last term, i.e., pretty in a blonde clichéd sort of way with a face that made it clear you had to have a good reason for daring to speak to her. I don't know why I thought she might be different after a summer cantering around the countryside, or whatever she did when she wasn't at Pankhurst. I tended to mute her on social media in the holidays, which was dangerous, of course. It would have been more sensible to keep an eye on her.

"Look, girls! It's our new House Prefect," said Clemmie. She stood up and applauded. The new first-formers sitting cross-legged on the rugs looked at each other, clearly wondering if this was a thing, and if they were expected to clap too. As Paige, a less shiny version of Clemmie with thinner hair and lips, laughed behind her hand, you could see them work it out: this was sarcasm.

I nodded at her, without smiling. I hoped it looked icily regal. It said: *Yes, I'm House Prefect. I know you wanted it to be you, but it's not. So. Suck. It. Up.*

General chatter in the room slowly resumed. Second-formers brought us small white bone-china plates, cakes on trays and dainty mugs of tea. As of tomorrow, tea would be self-service in Pankhurst dining hall.

There was a buzz in the room at first-day tea with around seventy-five girls crammed into the room. Everyone was there apart from the sixth-formers at Davison, who would join us for dinner later. New girls watched established ones. People exchanged news from the last nine weeks of summer. They grumbled about rooms, and pulled apart cakes to check for raisins. Past wrongs were remembered.

Meribel scraped a lump of thick buttercream off a slice of chocolate cake with a teaspoon and moulded it in to a ball between her thumb and forefinger. "Did I tell you Paige walked off with my Miracle Kingdom lip liner in the last games lesson of term?"

"Yes, many times," I said.

"She pretended she had one just like it," said Meribel. "Nuh. It's a limited edition and you can't even buy it in this country."

"Go ahead, Bel. Fire," I said. "She deserves it."

"She'll lob it back," said Lo, eying the buttercream missile. "Let's see what the new housemistress is like before you get into a food fight."

"Chill," I said to Lo. It wasn't that she was gutless. Just more cautious than Meribel and me.

Meribel placed the buttercream ball in the teaspoon, lined up her shot and flicked it across the room. It hit Paige's arm with a speed and accuracy she never displayed in games lessons.

Paige made a squealing sound. Ms Calding didn't notice. We saw Paige take a bit of non-bake brownie and squish it into ammunition. If the greasy piece of cake had landed anywhere other than Meribel's hair, that would have been that, but her hair was sacred.

Meribel scraped a bigger lump of buttercream and hurled it towards Paige, who dodged. It landed on the velvet upholstery, and there were shocked murmurs from some of the first-formers.

Ms Calding strode across to the sofa, and then spun in our direction. "Who threw that?"

The chatter dimmed and Meribel kept quiet.

Ms Calding asked again in a louder voice, leaving half a pause between each word. She was going about this the wrong way, picking a fight in front of the whole house.

Besides, it was an unwritten law of Pankhurst: no one ever snitched.

"Nobody saw," said Clemmie and sipped her tea, keeping her eyes on Calding like a challenge, to see what she would do.

Calding stood up straighter. "If it happens again, there will be consequences." She walked towards the mantelpiece, which, being in the centre of the room, was the natural place to deliver the predictable news that things were going to change with her at the helm. She turned her head slowly as she spoke, first one way and then the other. There was something not quite Mount Norton about her attitude, as if she didn't believe we'd ever turn out to be the Creative and Original Thinkers of Tomorrow we were regularly promised that we would become in assemblies.

"D'you think her head swivels all the way round?" I muttered, barely moving my lips.

Lo gave a snort and Calding's eyes were on her immediately.

"I am combining my duties as housemistress with covering some science classes, so you may see me around the school," she said, "but my main priority is getting this boarding house back on track, and I'm going to need your help with that."

The younger girls smiled politely. The rest of us waited.

"I shall be pinning up the rules in the hallway, so you can become fully acquainted with them." She waved the

15

pile of papers that she was holding. How many sheets *were* there?

I leaned back against my chair and absent-mindedly ran my finger along my nose. From across the room, Clemmie caught my eye and a slight smile appeared. I sat up straight again. I was Kate Jordan-Ferreira. I was House Prefect, not her. She had more Instagram followers than anyone else in the school because she put a lot of work into her pouty photos and pathetic words of inspo, but her online fans didn't know what she was like in real life.

Calding waited until there was absolute silence before she began speaking again, this time about some maintenance issues with the building that hadn't finished during the summer. I zoned out as I contemplated something far more critical: as House Prefect, it was up to me to plan a decent illegal party for a select group from all seven boarding houses. Pankhurst usually threw the best ones, so I had a reputation to keep up. Not only this, by general agreement the boarding houses rotated the order in which the parties were held, and this year it was Pankhurst's turn to kick off the party season.

When I was panicking in Italy about this, Lo had reminded me about the unexpectedly successful party I'd had in the third form, only a couple of terms after I'd started at Mount Norton. Mucking around on the beach, we'd discovered one of the beach huts had a broken lock and it was empty. As it wasn't far off my birthday,

I suggested to Meribel and Lo that we return with fairy lights, portable speakers and snacks a couple of nights later. It was April and the weather was unseasonably warm. It turned into a party, with people hearing about it and turning up. There was midnight paddling (which became skinny dipping in people's imaginations when they recalled it later), alcohol, and stories about things happening behind the beach huts which may or may not have been true. It gave me a certain standing in Mount Norton. I went from being the new girl to the girl who'd had the beach hut party. It had been a pivotal moment for my popularity, although I wasn't stupid; I knew my looks helped too.

Veronica, last year's House Prefect, had come up with the perfect venue for the Pankhurst party: the flat roof of the beach café. We'd accessed it by climbing up a pile of crates and wheelie bins; the café was only one storey high. Veronica and her friends had positioned hundreds of tea lights in jars around the roof and had set up a cocktail bar. Our locked Instagram accounts were full of amazing photos.

The Pankhurst party was widely considered to be the best of the year. Monro, a boy in the year above, broke a bone in his ankle jumping down from the roof, but he managed to hobble off without getting any adults involved. There was also a kiss I regretted, and then later there was the whole thing about Sasha, but I didn't want to think about that either.

17

Calding hit her stack of papers against her hand to emphasize some point she was making. This talk looked as if it might go on a while.

Fingers crossed, I'd have the party sorted soon. During the last couple of weeks of the summer holiday I'd been in touch with my godfather, Steve, and a plan was coming together for my party. Although it was my idea, I couldn't do it without his help. A wild friend of my father's from university, Steve was someone who dipped in and out of my life, throwing around extravagant gestures before disappearing again. He once arrived unannounced at Elsie Gran's house in the back of a limo to take me out for dinner. Another time, he sent a delivery of fourteen helium balloons, each with a different sparkly letter printed on them. I eventually worked out they spelled LOTS OF LUCK KATE: he'd heard I was doing the entrance exam for Mount Norton.

A property on the clifftop had recently been listed on Airbnb, and I was still waiting to hear if he could rent it for a weekend, for my party. He didn't need to pay for it – I had savings for that – but he insisted, saying it would make up for a few missed birthdays and Christmases. I'd chosen the date of the Mount Norton Autumn Party, a compulsory school social which always ended early, and meant everyone would be free afterwards. He'd emailed to ask for my assurance that it wouldn't be trashed under my care, and I replied that I'd do my best. He'd found that amusing, and said he'd send on the bill for any repairs.

I'd passed the house many times when running along the coastal path. I'd seen huge rectangles of glass arrive on a lorry one weekend morning in the spring, and afterwards I'd heard Wibbz tell Squirrel she'd had it on good authority from someone in the village that the kitchen had been made specially and was coming over from Denmark.

The photos on the website showed bedrooms with floor-to-ceiling windows, and a large reception room with huge doors that folded back so you could walk out into the sandy, landscaped garden with pale pebbles of identical size and clumps of thick grass, surrounded by a low white fence. It was the sort of house you saw in movies set in California. It was literally perfect. Even if it rained it would be perfect – I pictured how we'd watch the storm out of the big windows and scream when the thunder broke and the lightning dazzled. My party would be jaw-dropping. I wanted to uphold Pankhurst's reputation as the best girls' boarding house, but I also wanted people to see I was capable of something daring and brilliant. I realized now how lucky I was to be going first with my party. Nailing it would mean being able to enjoy the rest of the year knowing I'd go down in Mount Norton history for the best of reasons.

The website showed a photo of the garden at night, soft light glowing from outdoor lamps, a bottle of wine and two glasses on the bleached-wood table. *Nothing but the sound of waves crashing on the shore below this clifftop oasis*, said the caption. *The ultimate getaway for those requiring peace and tranquillity.*

Ha.

I would tell Meribel and Lo as soon as it was confirmed. I couldn't wait to see their faces. After that I'd leak the news gradually to the people on our guest list, who might not necessarily be the people we wanted to come. It was the way it worked though: Mount Norton parties relied on exclusivity to have any chance of success.

I ate another square of lemon drizzle cake. Squirrel was a consistently good cook, unlike my grandmother. Elsie Gran had cooking frenzies with fruit and vegetables from her allotment, but then had times when cooking bored her, and it would be nothing but omelettes for days on end unless I took over. Her favourite food was Sultana Bran, and plain biscuits which she dunked into black coffee while momentarily holding her cigarette in the other hand. This summer, after coming back from Italy, I'd had a go at making almond biscotti, and she'd loved them. I'd made a triple batch before leaving for Mount Norton this morning.

Calding had moved on to other notices. She read out a list of clubs and societies which would be running this term. Everyone was to make sure they used the recycling bins around the house. The winner of the Pankhurst Art Award had been won by Veronica Steepleton. Her name would go up in gold lettering on the art awards plaque in the assembly hall in the main school, and the winning artwork was already on display in Davison common room.

I wasn't surprised Veronica had won, but the desire to win it myself this year vibrated through my ribs. I would do a sculpture. As far as I knew, a sculpture had never won.

Ms Calding looked down at her notes again. "It says here that the winner receives five thousand pounds. Has that been written down wrong?"

There was a general shout out that five thousand was right and Calding pulled her head back slightly, with the momentary shock you sometimes saw on people's faces when Mount Norton surprised them with its casual wealth.

The fees for the school were among the highest in the country. There were scholarship students, of course, and those whose fees were paid by their parents' employers, but not many. The amount of our individual allowances varied hugely though. We didn't discuss them but we knew who was able to afford expensive things and who wasn't. My parents paid a lot of money sporadically into my bank account rather than set up regular payments, and I hated asking for more when it ran out.

Elsie Gran sent me a five-pound note every week, sandwiched between sections of Sultana Bran cardboard so it couldn't be seen through the envelope. When I was living with her, she left them under an old clock I had in my bedroom.

Elsie Gran refused financial help from my parents because she didn't approve of my father making money through what she said were *other people's insecurities*, and she

21

never had a good word to say about my mother. She barely approved of me, but the first time I'd gone to live with her was a week after her cat of fifteen years died, and she told me I'd filled a void, and at least I didn't bring in half-dead mice or birds.

Something hit the side of my cheek, and when I touched it I knew it was cake, sticky against my skin. Across the room, Paige was studying her nails, and Clemmie was yawning. Her yawn looked suspiciously as if she was laughing at me. There had been quiet in the room but now there was absolute stillness. Everyone in the room, apart from Paige, had their eyes on me. Never before had anyone dared to humiliate the House Prefect like this. I could storm out, but that would be seen as weakness and Clemmie and Paige would love that. I pushed down the anger for now, and concentrated on wiping my cheek with a napkin, pretending to do it absent-mindedly while listening to Calding's boring speech. But she'd stopped.

"Who threw that?" she said.

Silence.

Mrs Haven, the assistant housemistress, who'd been standing by the door, shifted uncomfortably. We called her the Ghost because she had white hair, wore beige and glided about without saying much.

Calding said, "Right," in such a loud voice, several first-formers shrank back. "Here is the consequence: no dessert tonight at dinner."

There was a collective gasp. The Ghost's mouth went

slack. First-night desserts tended to be pretty good.

Calding tucked a lock of lank hair behind her ear.

"That's so unfair," whined a third-former.

"I said there would be consequences," Calding said in a tight voice. "You are now dismissed. I'll see everybody later at dinner."

We stood up and shuffled to the door, and the Ghost gave little smiles to us, like you might if there'd been an accident and you were trying to put a brave face on it.

"Squirrel is going to hate her," said Lo as we hoofed it up the stairs. "All those wasted desserts."

"Everyone's going to hate her," I said.

Clemmie was ahead of us, making her way up to the second floor where the rest of the fifth-formers had their rooms in either single or twin rooms. "Pre-drinks in my room, anyone?" she called.

She didn't mean me, Lo or Meribel. She knew we wouldn't go even if she asked us. She didn't mean Zeta either, who had a collection of furry gnome things on display and never hid her appalling homesickness, or the twins who did nothing but study or practise their musical instruments. She meant the girls who would have taken a bullet for Clemmie, or at least a detention.

"Pre-drinks *on my terrace*, anyone?" I murmured to Lo and Meribel.

CHAPTER 3

There was no sun on the fire escape at this time of day, but the metal transmitted gentle warmth, and the sky was what I thought of as coastal blue. I produced three low-slung outdoor chairs from my trunk, which had been brought up by the premises team while we'd had tea and been lectured. We rarely saw the premises staff, who only called in at the boarding houses when required for heavy lifting or maintenance jobs.

I had vodka in a shampoo bottle, and some cute shot glasses I'd bought in an Italian market, patterned with a silvery tree design. I rationed out a tiny bit of vodka for each of us, and added Diet Coke. The chairs were pretty comfortable, though it took some effort for us to lean forward in them enough to clink glasses and drink to the new school year.

"Tell us what progress you've made with the Pankhurst party," said Meribel after we'd taken our first sip.

"I've got a plan. I don't want to tell you in case it doesn't come off, but I'll know soon."

Lo gave a little sitting-down dance. "Oooooh."

"You're teasing us," said Meribel. "Come on. Spill."

I shook my head. "Nope. Not yet." I pointed at the railing to the right of the fire escape. "I reckon if I stood against that and leaned forward I could see..." I placed my glass down, stood up and tried it. "Yes! You can see over the trees. There's the tennis court and, look, a bench. Good spying opportunities!"

Meribel and Lo stood next to me. It wasn't our tennis court. It belonged to Churchill, the next-door boarding house for boys, which was a far grander building and had extensive grounds. Each of the four boarding houses for boys was larger than any of the three for girls. Wibbz said it was because Mount Norton had started off as a single-sex school, and when girls were admitted, there hadn't been suitable buildings of comparable size for them. I didn't see why the girls couldn't swap a building with the boys, or why the school still took in more boys than girls. I'd heard a rumour that when Miss Sneller was appointed headteacher five years ago, a family had removed their sons because they didn't want a female in charge. It might wow visitors with its location and facilities, but this school wasn't the forward-thinking place it liked to think it was.

"We'll be able to see more when the leaves fall," I said as we dropped down on to our chairs again.

"That sounds stalkery," said Meribel.

I rolled my eyes.

"And Bernard isn't even at Churchill," said Lo.

"Stop!" I said. "I'm done with you two winding me up about Bernard."

Meribel said, "But I love talking about him. It makes me laugh."

"That kiss was a mistake," I said. "How many times have I told you that?"

"OK, OK," said Meribel, smirking.

Lo touched the silvery tree on the side of her shot glass. "Speaking of mistakes... There was this girl on the campsite..."

"And?" said Meribel.

"Tell us *everything*," I said.

Lo pushed the fingers of one hand back with her other. It was a nervous thing that drove Meribel and me mad. We ignored it this time, because we were too interested in what she had to say. Lo said, "We were in her tent, and she took my phone and I was trying to get it back off her, and we ended up kissing, but it didn't feel right. And it kind of... It made me realize how much I miss Sasha."

Sweat gathered at the back of my neck. I would let this conversation happen without me. Or, if I had

26

to join in, I would carefully nudge it in a different direction.

Lo looked at me and then Meribel. "I hate coming back to school and her not being here."

"Of course you're going to miss her," said Meribel. "You were together for. . ."

"Four-and-a-half months," said Lo. "Nearly five."

"You're only remembering the good things about her," said Meribel. "Remember what she did."

Lo didn't say anything.

"You can tell a lot from a kiss," I said, hoping Meribel would take the bait and lead the conversation elsewhere. She did.

"You've only ever kissed Bernard," she said.

"And I learned a lot," I said. "I'm ready for Hugo now."

At precisely the same time, Meribel and I said, "You saw Janetta's post?" then laughed at our synchronicity. Hugo was one-hundred-per-cent the best-looking guy in the whole of Mount Norton, and happened to be in the same year as us. He was also super-smart and sporty. He'd be going to an Ivy League American university one day; we all knew it. Meribel and I were following his girlfriend, Janetta, who went to another school, on social media, and she'd posted over the summer about their messy break-up.

I absolutely knew a kiss with Hugo would be radically different to the one I'd had with Bernard at the beach café party.

27

Bernard hadn't even been someone on my list of would-like-tos. A group of us had been playing Never Have I Ever on the roof of the café, and Clemmie was challenging someone's answer, accusing them of lying. Bernard, who was sitting cross-legged next to me, had told her it was only a stupid drinking game, but she wouldn't let it go, and the rest of us had become bored. Bel, Lo and Sasha hadn't been playing because they'd wanted to dance on the concrete walkway, which we called the promenade. I decided to join them, clambering down from the roof via the bin. I'd stood watching for a moment in the shadow of the porch, waiting for a better song to come on, and Bernard joined me. I felt desirable that night. I wanted to be kissed. I was Kate Lynette Jordan-Ferreira, nearly sixteen, and I'd never kissed anyone properly. It had to change, and Bernard was right there, murmuring that he'd fancied me hard since I joined the school. He was a bit of an idiot, and he wasn't Hugo, but he was there and wanted to kiss me.

He pressed his mouth on mine and his tongue was thick and insistent, and I couldn't lose myself in the moment even though I tried. I filtered out the lyrics of the song which was playing, and the laughter and chatter. I couldn't seem to cross into a different way of being. The only sensation I felt was of fleshiness in my mouth, and of his hand pressed hard against my back. It wasn't what I thought it would be.

Meribel's voice cut into my thoughts. "Nearly time for the Ghost to go home," she said, tapping me on my arm with her phone. "She was on the early shift. I'll film if you like. My phone's brand new. The camera's incredible."

Most times, the Ghost left by the back gate and her husband picked her up in his car in the back lane. The gate had a PIN code on it which was changed every term. We'd learned, along with a few other people in Pankhurst, that it was possible to take a video of the Ghost leaving and zoom in later to read the code. The first few times the Ghost inputted the code in a new term, she did it slowly, which was helpful.

We moved the chairs inside, and Meribel knelt by the open window. "Her husband better be picking her up this evening," she said. "I don't want her going out of the front door and taking the bus. Wait. Shhh. There she is."

Lo and I stood well back so we wouldn't be seen gawping if the Ghost happened to look up, though I suspected her eyesight wasn't that good even if she did.

"Got it," said Meribel. "I'm pretty sure it's one nine eight four." She stood up and we watched over her shoulder as she replayed the video. "Yep. Right, I'm deleting it now. Guard it closely, guys. What next? Davison common room?"

It took us ten minutes to get ready, and just over five minutes to get from the third floor, out of the front door and across the road to swipe into Davison with our fifth-form cards. The common room was on the ground floor. We breezed in. It was huge and modern compared to the junior common room in Pankhurst, and was rammed with students, a mixture of fifth- and sixth-formers. There was a corner sofa with fluffy cushions, and some comfy chairs nearby. Naturally Clemmie had hogged a spot on the corner sofa. Her friends were bunched round her, trading gossip. There were lots of white tables and chairs in the centre of the room. A pool table was at one end, a kitchen area at the other.

Davison was the common room to hang out in.

"Hey!" Bernard appeared in a T-shirt that announced he'd done a 10k run for charity. "How are you lovely lot?"

"We're lovely, thanks," said Meribel.

I managed a half-smile, and wondered when I would stop feeling awkward around him. At least we'd sort of got back to being friendly. After our kiss last term, when I'd made it clear I didn't want anything more, he hadn't spoken to me for at least two weeks, but it had gradually become less uncomfortable. This new friendliness was going to take some getting used to though.

Lo had ordered a picture book for me as a joke at the end of last term. It was called *Not Now, Bernard*. The book's Bernard had parents who ignored him repeatedly, saying "Not now, Bernard", and in the end a monster ate him.

"Where did you summer?" Bernard asked. His use of summer as a verb made me want to throttle him. I let Meribel talk about Berlin, and he butted in to tell us about his incredible time in South-East Asia. As he unlocked his phone to show us a photo of a waterfall he'd trekked to, Lo mouthed, *Not now, Bernard*.

I widened my eyes at her and she stifled a giggle. After Lo had left our villa in Italy, my mother had said, "What a quiet friend you have." Meribel, on the other hand, was more the sort of person my mother would love if they ever met – loud, impulsive and very fashion-conscious, from a family who'd made a lot of money and weren't afraid of what Elsie Gran called *conspicuous spending*. Lo was one of the cleverest people in our year, and amazing at dance. She spent a good proportion of her life on YouTube watching dance routines, which she absorbed as easily as her revision notes. She was outwardly more reserved than me and Meribel, and you had to know her well before she'd show you her fun side.

Meribel swivelled around as Bernard was in full flow and muttered, "Hugo's here."

I looked immediately and heard Meribel tut at my unsubtlety. He looked better than ever: tanned, relaxed and wearing perfect-fit jeans.

"Hiya, Hugh!" called Clemmie from the sofa in a baby voice. "Come and sit with us on the sofa." They lived near each other in the same part of Sussex. There was a whole clique at Mount Norton who'd been to the same prep school and whose parents all socialized together. Veronica and Monro, the ankle-breaker, were part of their home crowd too.

Hugo spoke to the whole room as he said, in a spot-on impression of Wibbz, "Oh my darlings – how happy I am to see your faces!" in exactly the way she would have if she'd been there.

Everyone laughed. I was determined to have him to myself for a few minutes before he reached Clemmie, so I stepped towards him and said, "I hope you're looking forward to this year's party challenge." We were both House Prefects, although technically, as his house had a sixth form as part of it, his title was House Prefect of the Lower School.

Hugo held my gaze. I felt a leap of excitement as I moved my head a fraction to show him my best side. I would do everything it took to impress him.

"Bring it on," he said. "May the best person win."

I smiled, and said, "Absolutely."

Clemmie called to him again, and he murmured, "Please excuse me," and moved on.

I didn't turn to watch him go. It would have been unsubtle, and I didn't want to see Clemmie embrace him.

I'd already been here in Davison for a dare when I was new, two years ago. I'd heard that Clemmie thought I was too full of myself, so I decided I'd do the initiation test she set for eager new students. I'd do an enhanced version of it. Clemmie had persuaded first-formers to find a way into Davison and stay as many minutes as they could before being chucked out by a sixth-former or an angry member of staff.

I decided I would pull an all-nighter.

Apparently most of the first-formers barged their way in as a sixth-former swiped in with their school card and so brought obvious attention to themselves. I strode in with some library books I'd nabbed from the main school library which needed to go across to the Davison one. They were easy to spot on the trolley as they had different coloured stickers. A passing teacher was only too happy to let a helpful library-loving third-former in. And then it was a matter of finding a hiding place, and keeping Wibbz from noticing I was missing. It was remarkably, disturbingly easy. Meribel had to spin some story about me being in the bathroom at one point but that was all.

I posted footage of myself in a cleaning cupboard and then in the common room, expecting to be thrown out any moment, but left at six in the morning when the cleaners arrived.

Clemmie said it had only worked because I was insignificant and nobody cared where I was. But she couldn't ignore the fact that the photos and videos of my Davison sleepover had been liked and viewed by our classmates more than anything she had ever posted, despite the number of followers she had.

I was aware of Lo beside me, saying something. She pointed and I saw a large, colourful collage of red, pink, purple and orange made from what looked like paper, fabric and paint: Veronica's artwork. People must have been standing in front of it before because I don't know how we'd have missed seeing it otherwise.

"Is it a sunset?" asked Meribel.

"Dunno," I replied and walked over to take a closer

look. There was a rectangle of something stitched on to red silk in the corner, a selfie that had been made to look like a Polaroid photo. It was of Veronica sitting next to Monro, her hand in her hair as if she'd been pushing it away from her face. The colours were bleached out and yellowy, but the two of them were laughing. A golden Mount Norton couple.

"That was taken about ten minutes before he did his ankle in," said Veronica. I hadn't noticed her in the room before then. She was holding a mug of tea, her hair in a high ponytail, wearing baggy red linen dungarees and a stripy purple-and-red bralette top, which Calding most definitely wouldn't approve of. In those colours, she could have walked into her own artwork and been camouflaged.

"It was such a cool party," said someone.

Veronica nodded, and turned to where Monro was crouched by the sink, looking into a cupboard. I didn't know if they were a proper couple, but they were tight.

People were wary of Monro. He was quiet but he was known to have anger issues. He'd punched a window in Churchill and had an ugly raised scar on his arm to show for it.

"M, you found any sugar yet?" Veronica called across the room at him.

He stood up. He'd become even taller over the summer. "Nope."

"Wibbz would have made sure we were stocked properly," Veronica said, and sighed. There was a separate housemistress for Davison but Wibbz had often done shifts to keep in touch with her former girls. "We should start a petition to get her back. We could crowdfund to send her off to Arizona or somewhere to dry out first?"

"There's no point," said Flo, one of Veronica's friends. "Nobody's parents are going to let her come back now they know she has a problem."

Before I moved away from the collage, I read the printed label at the side of the artwork, black writing on white paper on grey board, the classy Mount Norton way. It said:

Mixed Media by Veronica Steepleton
Title: The Things We Keep Hidden

CHAPTER 4

There was quiet, seething resentment at dinner from both girls and kitchen staff due to the dessert situation. Squirrel stood by the whiteboard menu with her thick, meaty arms folded, muttering in Bulgarian. The main course options were Mediterranean chicken casserole and vegetarian stir-fry, but all casseroles were known as Squirrel stew and tended to taste the same. She was a big fan of black olives and tomato puree. The dessert options – lemon meringue pie, profiteroles and Eton mess – had been crossed through with a red marker instead of being erased.

The walls of the dining hall were lined with dark wood panels. There were several portraits in ornate gilt frames. One of them was of Emmeline Pankhurst, the boarding house's namesake, but the largest by far was of the boarding-house founder, a woman who looked humourless and grumpy. Calding and the Ghost patrolled the dining hall like prison wardens. We had to sit where we could. Apparently it was no longer allowed for me as House Prefect to reserve a table. When I asked why, Calding said it wasn't on the designated list of privileges. It was only something her predecessor had allowed.

"But Wibbz turned it into a tradition," I said.

"Pankhurst is going back to basics with rules," said Calding. Her eyes didn't flinch from mine. She didn't care about being liked, that was certain.

"I'm going to complain to Miss Sneller," I said.

"I'm sure the head has much more serious things to worry about at the start of the new term, don't you?" Calding said.

We ended up on a shared table with some third-formers and Zeta. Zeta listened to our conversation about plans for decorating our rooms, and didn't say anything until Lo asked how she was, and her eyes welled up with tears, and she said, "I'm fine," in her squeaky little voice. How could she get to the fifth form and still be so hopelessly homesick? She told us how she'd had a photo of her hamster printed on to a cushion so she could snuggle up with him in bed.

"Disturbing," murmured Meribel. I smiled politely at Zeta. She could do so much more to fit in at Pankhurst. It was hard not to be irritated by her.

The rest of the evening was ahead of us – supposedly for board games, music practice, yoga in Davison or "screen time" (as if none of us had second phones, in addition to the ones that were ceremoniously brought out of the locked cupboard in the front office for screen time).

First off, I called Elsie Gran with my earphones in so I could finish unpacking while I spoke to her.

"Katelyn!" She was the only person who called me that, mashing my first name with my middle name, Lynnette.

"Missing me?" I asked.

"Not yet," said Elsie Gran. She could be brutal like that, but I noted she'd picked up the phone on the first ring. "Everything OK?"

"Uh-huh," I said. I lifted Blu Tack and some carefully selected photos from my bag of fragile items, which had been at the top of my trunk. "The new housemistress is mean, but hopefully she won't be here long."

"Must be hard working in a school full of over-entitled kids," said Elsie Gran.

"We're not all over-entitled," I said.

Elsie Gran snorted. She told me Maria next door had invited her round the next day to see the first couple of episodes of a new Netflix series, and did I want to know what happened in the end in the audiobook we'd been listening to on the way to Mount Norton.

I listened to her deep voice more than her words. It always made me feel calmer. Her view of the world was so certain.

Five minutes later, the evening began properly. Meribel, Lo and I lay on Meribel's bed watching a new K-pop video, and then Lo made us get up and see if we could remember a dance routine she'd taught us last term. We got as far as a fast turn, which I overdid and sidestepped in the wrong direction, making the others laugh so much they stopped. We started again, turning up the music louder than we'd have got away with if we'd been on the floors below.

Eventually we'd had enough, and I said, "We should go to the beach tonight."

Wibbz had rarely made it up the first flight of stairs to say goodnight to us. Calding would be different, but she couldn't patrol all night. To repeatedly check on students in bed would be weird.

Going out on the first night would show the rest of Pankhurst I wasn't afraid of Calding. I was House Prefect. Veronica was a hard act to follow, so I had to be fearless. Clemmie would be out tonight, I was sure of that, so I would be there too, taking a few photos for evidence.

"I don't think I should go," said Lo. "Calding's genuinely strict. If I'm suspended it's going to wreck my chance of a scholarship next year." She did the pushing-back-of-her-fingers thing, and let her springy copper hair fall forward to curtain half her face. In a quieter voice, she added, "Sorry."

I sighed heavily. "Oh, come on," I said. "I'm sure loads of other people are going to be there; it's not that big a deal if we get caught." At this rate, she'd be refusing to come to my beach house party, which would be unthinkable.

Lo pushed back her hair to look at me. "I'm not going."

I wanted us to be closer than we'd ever been, a force to be reckoned with. It wasn't starting off well. "Suit yourself," I said brusquely, and I caught the hurt in her eyes before she went towards the door.

"I'm going to unpack," she said, and left the room.

Meribel shrugged at me. "She'll loosen up as the term gets going." She lifted her hands to redo her hair, twirling it up into a bun, expertly tucking the end in. "I've got a few work calls to make. There's something in the pipeline, and I need to find out more."

"What sort of thing?" I asked.

"A shoot in Japan," said Meribel. She sashayed across the room like a model, then jazz-handed her excitement. "A. Mazing. Yeah?" One of the reasons she hated Clemmie so much was that Clemmie once said Meribel only got modelling work because she had "an unusual face" that ticked the diversity card. Clemmie was so full of it, the jealous wannabe.

As Meribel struck ridiculous poses to make me laugh, I had the sensation of facing the wrong direction. It hadn't occurred to me she'd contemplate going off so early in the school year, not now we had third-floor status and exams.

"I'll have to beg Sneller for time off if it happens," said Meribel, draping herself across the bed. "That's always tedious."

If she wasn't given permission, she'd go anyway. The head usually gave it retrospectively.

"But it's the beginning of term," I said, my voice sounding like a wail.

She laughed – she thought I was being ironic.

Calding came lightly up the stairs at nine thirty-six, when I was reading in bed.

After knocking on my door, Calding waited half a second before walking in, her eyes flicking round the room. She took in the photos, of me, Lo and Bel, and one of Elsie Gran, back before I was born, on a march against nuclear energy. Elsie Gran was mid-shout and looked as determined as anyone I'd seen, ready to take on the world. This was the first year I hadn't put one up of my parents. I'd finally allowed myself not to. They didn't have any photos of me in their house. When I'd pointed this out to my mother, she hadn't missed a beat. She said family photos weren't her thing. She pointed out there were none of my father either. Neither of us mentioned the enlarged photo of herself on the wall of the reception room that led outside to the terrace, protected from the sunshine by a white canopy. That was different because it was art.

"Making yourself at home?" said Calding. She spoke with forced cheeriness. I bet this was her first house mistress job, but I also bet if I asked her, she wouldn't tell me.

"Getting there," I said. It was uncomfortable having her in my room.

"So," began Calding. She pulled her thumb and forefinger over the corners of her mouth, as if to remove the spit that might be resting there. "I hope as House Prefect you will be an example to Pankhurst students this year."

"Of course," I said lightly. I would be a shining example of how to live the best House-Prefect life.

"Lights out at ten-thirty," said Calding. "Sleep well." As she left the room, I noticed she'd changed the heeled shoes she'd been wearing earlier for flat espadrille-type shoes with a rubber sole. I didn't like the idea of Calding gliding around as silently as the Ghost.

Meribel and I waited an hour and a quarter after Calding's night round before climbing out on to the fire escape, our convenient new way to leave the building. As I pulled the window back down behind us, I thought of Lo in her room, and regretted my harshness.

Meribel told me the first time she'd sneaked out at night, it had been with a girl who was now in Clemmie's friendship group, and they'd paid a fifth-former for the gate code. The traditional escape route was through the bathroom window on the first-floor corridor, on to the flat roof of the music room and down on to the courtyard paving. The window lock had been sorted so it looked as if it was locked when it wasn't.

It had seemed the most exciting thing ever when I'd been shown it by Meribel and Lo. I was totally up for illicit paddling in the moonlight, but the English Channel was so cold that night, it made us scream with pain. I was scared of the silhouettes of scrubby trees growing on the cliff face, and hated the pebbles, which were difficult to walk on, and the fact I couldn't see what was hopping or crawling over the damp sand by the water's edge. The murky water itself was not only bitingly cold, but filled with manky vegetation and God knows what else that brushed up against my bare skin. But the taste of danger was intoxicating.

We'd prepared for tonight's drop in temperature, and were wearing jeans, thick T-shirts and trainers. There was enough light from the moon and the street lights not to need our phone torches. I'd been listening out for the clicking noise of the back gate being opened, and hadn't heard anything so it was probable – and highly satisfying – that we were ahead of Clemmie and her crew.

At Pankhurst, the housemistress accommodation was on the ground floor, a collection of rooms behind the office. We couldn't see any lights showing, other than the usual night-lights which switched off automatically in the morning.

There was a fixed CCTV camera on the fence, which had been knocked at some point to make it possible to avoid being seen by climbing on the outside of the railings. We knew the technique at Churchill was to throw a jumper or other item of clothing over the cameras, but our way was more sophisticated. The steps were clanky, some more than others. I went first, cringing at every sound, and Meribel followed. At the bottom was a chain with its attached notice facing outwards: *Out of bounds.*

I let Meribel punch in the PIN code on the gate since she'd procured it for us. There was a slight delay until it clicked. I could suddenly taste salt in the air. We slipped through as quickly as we could, punching the air with the giddiness of freedom.

We headed down the lane. The quickest way to the beach, and the beach café, was down the wide zigzag path at the corner of the large car park at the end of the lane. It wasn't a path that encouraged walking. It was best gone down at speed with our arms out like five-year-olds pretending to fly. We slowed up at the bottom, when we reached the promenade. The café was shuttered up for the night, but Kipper, who ran it, had forgotten to bring in a sign advertising a new coconut-flavoured ice cream. It flapped noisily in the sea breeze. The steel door of the toilet block was locked but the tiny windows at the top were open, wafting out the stink. Further down the walkway the beach huts loomed.

We whooped to see the beach empty, and picked our way carefully across the pebbles and the small stretch of damp sand studded with stones, to stare at the dark incoming water edged with foam as it rolled in.

"Let's walk along on a groyne," said Meribel. The groynes, made from wood, were low walls which stretched out into the sea to keep the beach from eroding. Slipping would mean falling into the cold, churning sea, to an unknown depth, and there was a lot of green stuff to slip on.

"All right," I said. We'd seen Veronica do it once at night. It had been stupid and brave of her, but we could match that. "Halfway."

"Halfway's good," agreed Meribel. "And the light's great for photos."

I went first, hauling myself up via one of the groyne's vertical posts. My trainers were new, too new for the beach, but they had a good grip. The section that stretched over the shore felt easy. If I fell here it would be fine. But as I walked further along the wooden structure, my stomach dropped away, and I thought of freezing water, my ruined phone, trainers and clothes stiff with salt. How cold did the water need to be before it induced a heart attack? I tried to focus on the dark wood, looking for raised bits of furry moss or seaweed. Distracted by a clump further ahead, I placed my foot down too confidently where I was. The skid of my trainer matched the lurch in my body. I had no control over the scream that came out of me. I jerked myself upright, waiting in that split-second to see if I'd overcorrected and would fall backwards.

I was still upright. I'd got away with it.

Somewhere behind me, Meribel swore. "Let's get a photo and turn back," she shouted.

I thought of Veronica walking so calmly to the middle. Kate Lynette Jordan-Ferreira would be the same. "I'll get to the next post," I called, but not too loudly, worried the act of releasing too much breath might unbalance me as I edged along sideways.

At the post I swivelled round a few degrees at a time, watching my feet. "Ready?" I called and lifted my head, my smile in place.

Meribel was leaning against a post, in an uncomfortable-looking crouched position, framing the shot. She knew how to take a good photo, as well as how to make the camera love her.

"Hey!" The sudden shout came out of nowhere and made me flinch. "HEY!"

Startled, Meribel turned slightly and lost her balance. She stumbled back with a high-pitched screech, into the water with a crashing splash.

CHAPTER 5

Clemmie. It was Clemmie who'd shouted. I could see her up the beach with Paige, Bernard, Hugo and a couple of other boys from our year. Each of them had their phones out and they were videoing or taking photos. Nobody was interested in how far along the groyne I had come. They were fixated on Meribel, who was shrieking about how cold the water was and how she'd dropped her phone and couldn't find it because the water was too dark. Clemmie could not have looked more delighted as she panned round the beach and then back to Meribel, although she appeared to be having difficulty holding her phone steady because she was laughing so much.

Hugo went to the water's edge and held out his hand for Meribel to grab on to. At least he was doing something to help, and although I felt sorry for Meribel, I thanked God it wasn't me Hugo was seeing in that state. Meribel was wailing about her phone and how she'd only had it a couple of weeks, but as she came out of the water she pulled at her T-shirt and made a snorting sound that might have been a kind of laughter. It was a tactic we often used at Mount Norton. Make light of the situation; don't show how much you care.

Even from where I was standing on the groyne, I could see she was shivering violently. Clemmie was still taking photos, and suddenly Meribel was doing a pose, holding her hands up against her face and pushing her chest out, just like a glamour model.

Bernard shouted, "I dare you to do a cartwheel on that beam, Kate," and the attention turned to me.

"Forget the cartwheel, she's too scared to move at all," said Paige.

"I dare *you* to do a cartwheel, Bernard," I shouted back. "Come on, let's see it. It should be easy on dry land."

He laughed. He was a jokey person but he hated making a fool of himself so I knew he wouldn't.

Hugo yelled, "Kate, chuck us your phone in case you fall in too. You're a long way out."

Good point, and catching was one of the many things

Hugo was good at. What was even better was Hugo paying me close attention. Although he was in my year, I'd never got to know him.

I reached into my jeans pocket with a smooth, careful movement and eased out my phone.

Everyone was watching me now. Clemmie was filming, no doubt hoping she'd catch me falling in, or losing my phone too. If nothing happened, I'd never see the footage. She certainly wouldn't want anything showing me and Hugo getting along so well. I held my phone tightly, rubbing my forefinger over the curved end. My case was averagely robust but not waterproof.

I hesitated for one final second before throwing. It was a slow, gentle underarm throw and Bernard leapt in front of Hugo at the last minute to catch it with one hand. He held it up, with an *oh-yeah* wiggle. That must have been a fluke. Bernard was no sporting legend.

"You going to thank me?" he shouted.

"Er ... thanks," I shouted, a lot less enthusiastically than if Hugo had caught it.

"Pleasure's all mine, darling," he called and threw it up in the air and caught it again, just to make me gasp.

"Where's Scholarship Girl?" shouted Paige. "Working her little Primark socks off?"

Meribel swore at Paige, and said, "I'm legit minutes away from hypothermia," and I moved a little faster along my wooden tightrope, inhaling the dankness of the green vegetation that clung to my trainers.

I saw Bernard look at my phone, at the lock screen photo of me with Bel and Lo.

"Cute," he said loudly. "Now, let's see what's going on in your life." He swiped and prodded.

What? He couldn't get beyond that thumbprint-protected screen ... could he?

If anyone got into my phone I would be vulnerable. It was my own foolish fault, and I would fix it as soon as it was back in my possession and nobody was with me. I jumped down from the groyne as soon as I was sure I'd land on the beach, and I ran to grab it from him.

"No need to snatch," said Bernard.

"Thanks," I muttered, placing the phone inside my bra. I put my arm round Meribel. "You need to get warmed up." I rubbed her back, alarmed by how cold she was.

"Kate's so rude," I heard Clemmie say behind us as I marched Meribel towards the path.

Bernard raced after us. "Let me walk you back."

Why couldn't it have been Hugo?

"We don't need you to," I said.

Bernard walked alongside, too close, and pretended to look mournful. "I want to protect you from whatever's out there."

"Suit yourself," I said.

"No problem," said Bernard, as if we'd asked him to come with us.

Meribel was shaking pretty violently, and kept up a low

50

moaning sound as she took each step across the pebbles. Her trainers were waterlogged and encrusted with sand, but she was refusing to go barefoot because of the prickly burrs on the beach.

As we made our way across the pebbles, Bernard kept up a long story about an aggressive monkey in Thailand. At the promenade, Meribel stopped to take off her trainers and inspect the blisters they'd given her, and then couldn't face wedging her feet in them again.

As we walked up the zigzag path, Bernard told us about a girl he'd met on holiday who'd lost her passport and money and how he'd saved the day by letting her use his phone and lending her money. "You're a real–life hero, Bernard," said Meribel in a shivery voice.

"I know," said Bernard. He was actually serious.

"How about you save the day again and carry these?" She swung the trainers towards him by the laces.

"Ew, no thanks," he said. He pointed at the only car in the car park. It was a dark green vintage sports car, and we could see the outline of two people sitting in the front. "Look who it is."

"Who?" I asked, as I took Meribel's trainers from her. They were super-heavy and smelled of a fish tank that needed cleaning.

"Monro and Veronica." Bernard was almost leaping with excitement. "Caught them in the act!"

"Really?" It looked to me as if they were just sitting in

the front seats. "I didn't think you were allowed to have cars at school."

He ignored me. "This is hilarious. Come on, we'll give them a shock." He broke away from us, which was fine by me.

Meribel and I moved very slowly across the car park because her wet jeans were so uncomfortable. "I can't look," I said, but I kept on looking as I saw Bernard about to knock on the rear windscreen to make Veronica and Monro jump. "He is so embarrassing."

Within a millisecond of Bernard thumping on the glass, Monro had leapt out of the car.

Bernard ran towards us like the big chicken he was. "Sorry, mate, couldn't resist."

Monro shook his head slowly, and Veronica pushed open her door then, and got out. "Hi." She looked past Bernard to us. "Paddling accident?" she asked Meribel.

"Pretty much," said Meribel. "I. Am. Freezing."

"Car's warm. Hop in," said Monro. "I'll drive you down the lane. You and Kate." He looked pointedly at Bernard. "No room for you."

"She'll make your seats all wet," said Bernard.

"Cheers for that, Bernard," said Meribel. She walked towards Monro. "I'd really like a lift, thanks."

I heard Veronica say, "Monro," as if she didn't want him to do it, but he pretended he hadn't heard.

"I've got an old blanket in the boot," he said, and went to open it. I didn't know anyone who drove round with as much stuff in the back of their car, and that included Elsie

Gran. He pulled out a grey rug covered in white dog hairs from an old holdall and held it out to Meribel. "Wrap that round yourself and sit on it."

She grabbed it. "Thanks."

"I'm going back to the beach, then," said Bernard, returning towards the path. "See you tomorrow. Don't worry, I won't mention the car." He gave a salute, and Monro said, "Tosser."

Monro lifted the front seat forward for us for us to climb into the tiny cracked-leather back seat. Bel and I squished together. The blanket seemed to take up a disproportionate amount of room, and the trainers smelled even worse in the confined space. I said, "Are there any seat belts?"

Veronica turned her head and said, "I assume that was a joke. Only in the front."

Monro placed the seat back down and, as I was directly behind it, I had to move my knees right up to my chest.

The engine didn't want to start. "It's OK," I said. "We can walk. It's not far."

Meribel thumped me.

"It always starts third or fourth time," said Monro, and sure enough on the fourth turn of the key, the engine roared. He looked across at Veronica, and I couldn't work out what he was attempting to communicate to her, but he seemed tense.

"Nice car," I said.

Monro looked at me through the rear-view mirror.

53

"Thanks. I inherited it from my grandad in the summer." He must have just passed his test.

"His grandad was lovely," said Veronica. "He taught us both how to drive on his farm when we were twelve."

"Yeah, and you got it much more quickly than I did," said Monro.

I let them reminisce about an old Land Rover they used to drive on the farm, and hugged Meribel close, trying to transmit some of my body warmth to her.

Monro parked up at Pankhurst back gate, and moved his seat forward so we could get out. As I climbed through the door I tripped over the front seat belt, and he gripped my arm, placing his other hand on my back. The pressure of his hold gave me a feeling of lightness, as if I might float off the ground.

"All right?" he said. "That seat belt's a pain."

I nodded. His expression was serious. I'd rarely seen him smile, and I had an urge to tickle him, just to see what it would do to his face.

"Keep the blanket for now, Meribel," he said.

"Careful up the fire escape," called Veronica from her seat, ducking her head to try and see us. "The third step from the top is dented and sometimes makes a loud noise if you don't tread on it right."

We crept into the courtyard and up the fire escape, climbing up the outside until we were clear of the camera before vaulting carefully over the rail. We avoided the third step and climbed back in through my window.

Meribel went to have a hot shower, and I lay on my bed and deleted the photo of the photo I'd taken on my phone at Elsie Gran's a couple of days ago for silly, sentimental reasons. I replayed the evening, altering the facts so it was Hugo who caught my phone and accompanied me and Meribel up the zigzag path. I pictured me bundling Meribel into Monro's car and walking back to Pankhurst with Hugo. I imagined him placing his arm around my back and clutching my upper arm like Monro had done. I could almost feel the breath-catching lightness in my body again.

CHAPTER 6

Gentle sun flooded through my curtains the next morning when I woke to my alarm – autumnal English sun. It was soothing. I didn't want my first thought to be Elsie Gran, but it was. It was always the same when I went somewhere new, except Mount Norton wasn't new. I rolled over to pick up my phone on the table beside me. No messages.

I sent her a photo of the view out of my window. She'd like that. She wouldn't be interested in the actual room itself. It was such luxury to have it all to myself after sharing for the previous two years, first in a room for four, and then last year with Lo.

I checked what had been posted online about last night. Clemmie and Hugo had uploaded videos of Meribel falling into the sea. Bernard had posted a series of stills, including one of Meribel posing with her nipples showing through her wet T-shirt, and there were countless memes tagging her. There was nothing about me. I couldn't even post a photo of myself as I didn't have any from last night.

Naturally, there were some lovely ones of Clemmie with the sea in the background, and standing on a rock with Hugo. There was a sickening caption about being besties and a row of pink double-hearts.

I got out of bed and took a photo of my mildly sandy trainers. Later I'd think of a caption along the lines of *Interesting times at the beach last night* to remind people I was there. I showered and got dressed in school uniform: grey skirt, white shirt with school logo and dark-green V-neck jumper, with name tapes sewn in with poor stitching by Elsie Gran or neat stitching by me. We didn't have to wear our grey blazers until we left the house. When the first breakfast bell went, I knocked on Meribel and Lo's doors. "Are you two even out of bed?" I called.

Meribel emerged coughing, saying the freezing seawater had made her ill, and we walked into Lo's room together. She was on her bed, fully dressed, scrolling on her phone. "I'm ready," she said. "Catching up on last night's dramas."

"Yeah," said Meribel. "I need to replace my phone and I don't think my trainers can be saved." She looked around. "Maybe I should have stayed behind and sorted my room instead. Yours is looking good, Lo."

Lo was on the edge of her bed now, crouched down, doing the laces on her black school shoes. "Thanks."

Meribel sprayed herself with the perfume on Lo's chest of drawers, then sniffed her wrists. "Hm, I think you've had this too long. It goes off, you know."

Lo shrugged as she stood up. "It smells OK to me. We can't all buy perfume whenever we want. Or new phones and trainers."

It rarely came between us, the scholarship thing, but when it did Meribel and I usually fell silent, embarrassed. I once told her I understood because of living with Elsie Gran so much of the year, and Lo had snapped, "Your parents have plenty of money. You don't understand what it's like to be at this school with no money." Meribel sometimes tried to joke her way out of it, or I attempted to lighten the mood, like I did this time, by saying, "Well, we know what to get you for your birthday."

"That's not the point," Lo replied. She lifted her hair up and let it fall back over her shoulders. "But, you know, new perfume would be good. I've got this tester I was given in the summer – I'll find it later. It smells soooo nice."

I bumped up against her on purpose, flicking her with my hip. The awkwardness was over. "Come on, you're making us late."

As we turned the corner for the last flight of stairs, we saw a bottleneck of girls waiting to go past Calding's uniform checkpoint.

"Whaaat?" said Meribel. "This is a joke, right? First day of school, and this happens?"

We unrolled our skirts. Calding appraised Lo intently then waved her through, Meribel was told to remove her nail varnish and her nose piercing by lesson time, and I was detained by Calding's arm shooting out and forming a barrier as I attempted to step past. Surely she wasn't going to make a fuss. I was House Prefect. I looked fine.

"Skirt," she said.

I looked down at my skirt. It was maybe hitched up on one side where I hadn't fully completed the unrolling process. I fiddled with it.

"Happy?" I said.

Calding's skin appeared stretched over her delicate features, as if there might not be enough of it to allow for expansion into a smile.

"You may go," she said.

"Thanks," I said, as neutrally as I could. I wasn't going to let anyone see her push me down.

As we headed to the dining hall, I heard a fourth-former say Calding had sent Clemmie back to change and for the rest of the week she had to report to the office for a uniform check before breakfast. It made me think the uniform checkpoint hadn't been such a terrible idea after all.

The sky was pale blue that morning, and there was enough sunshine for us to wear sunglasses, because everyone looks better in sunglasses. We took off our blazers as soon as we were out of sight of Pankhurst, and walked in a row. Bel, me and Lo. Walking to school took a quarter of an hour if you went the most direct way, and five minutes of that was walking down the long driveway. The grounds were extensive, hidden by centuries-old brick walls in some parts, and newer fencing in others. Mount Norton was private in both senses of the word. The main building was mainly constructed from grey stone. It was part stately home, part cathedral and part modern extension. There were huge arched stained-glass windows in the assembly hall and stripped-back décor in the new part. From some of the classrooms on the first floor you could see the sea, and count the yachts heading towards the Isle of Wight.

Mount Norton was known for its excellent art and music provision, and there was a dedicated arts wing in the extension. It was so dramatic it often made visitors gasp – it's what made me agree to come here in the first place. The art rooms had been situated to make the most of natural light and the music rooms were soundproofed. It was possible to learn pretty much any instrument, and the music-tech kit was said to be on a level with professional studios. The art resources were seemingly infinite. We had our own pottery studio and dark room, and technicians who'd all been to art school.

I would have spent all day in the art rooms if I could. I had got into ceramic sculpture last year, enjoying the way it totally absorbed me. I produced a series of dragon-like creatures, which reared up on hind legs, or curled up but still remained watchful. They had large wings and fierce expressions. I'd brought one of them home for Elsie Gran, who positioned it on the mantelpiece in the living room straightaway. The rest of them stayed at school on their own shelf in one of the display cabinets, and I liked the idea they watched over me in the art room.

The initial assembly of the year was always particularly long and tedious, mitigated only by everybody eying each other up after the holidays. There were about a thousand of us in the assembly hall, and many things could happen over a long summer. Acne could clear up, breasts volumize, braces disappear and teeth whiten. A fabulous haircut could change everything.

We sat in year groups. Bernard, who was two rows in front of us, winked when he looked round and we made eye contact.

"Did he just *wink* at you?" murmured Meribel.

I nodded, and she giggled, and Lo leaned over me to ask what was so funny, and Mr Robertson our form tutor glared at us.

Monro, in the same row as Bernard, turned and mouthed, *You OK?* at Meribel. She nodded, then sneezed, and he jolted back, pretending the force of the sneeze had hit him. I laughed out loud, and he turned again. Was that a half-smile?

I looked around for Hugo. He turned out to be further down my row, which was irritating. It meant I couldn't observe him unless I leaned forward and made it really obvious.

The theme of the assembly was about starting the year with a clean slate, or *tabula rasa,* as Miss Sneller kept saying in Latin. We got the picture. We certainly didn't need it expanded over ten whole minutes and given the gravitas of a TED talk. I felt unpleasant pressure against my back, and spun round. Clemmie was motionless, looking intently at Miss Sneller, our headteacher, the knee that had jammed into my back suspended in the air.

"Stop," I said.

Mr Robertson moved swiftly and hissed at me. "Do you want me to send you out, Kate?"

I shook my head, and sat on the edge of my seat, pushing my shoulder blades together, then stretching my arms, one then the other, just to give myself something to focus on, and with the added benefit of blocking Clemmie's view, and giving her what might be construed as the middle finger. I was rotating a shoulder blade when Ms Calding came on to the stage and I realized the motivational speech was over.

Calding was being officially introduced, along with other new members of staff. The others were smiling, but Calding was gazing round the hall, as if she'd never seen anything like it. It was awe-inspiring with the wooden panelling, stained glass and, behind a Perspex screen, a faded tapestry that dated back to the fourteenth century, depicting men on horseback with swords and a fat angel resting on the clouds above them. Calding was asked to talk about her role but I'd heard it all before and switched off, admiring the ornate carved-wood ceiling instead.

When the spotlight had moved to the new maths teacher, who wore a patchwork waistcoat so awful it was genius, Calding's eyes darted about among the crowd, no doubt checking for misbehaving Pankhurst students.

"That woman is looking right at me. She's deranged," I heard Clemmie mutter behind me. For once I agreed with her, but it didn't stop me pushing my chair back with sudden force when I stood up as soon as assembly was over, right into her kneecaps.

CHAPTER 7

Fittingly, the history department was in the old part of the school. My classroom had stone flooring, a large oak door with a shiny brass handle, and heavily scented flowers in a jug in an alcove. The flowers were a typical Nortonian touch, and were changed daily unless someone with violent hayfever complained, in which case they were replaced by a sculpture.

Seating plans were the bane of my life, although they occasionally meant I heard school gossip that I might otherwise have missed. No such luck with Tessa Malone, who I'd been assigned to sit next to for the second year running. She only liked to talk about reality TV stars, a few of whom she'd met because her dad was big in film finance.

Some of them followed her on Instagram and she'd been to a few parties in secret locations, i.e. warehouses. Big deal. She was also bad at history, which made sitting next to her even more pointless. She was, however, popular at Mount Norton because she seemed to be able to persuade her parents to order anything and have it delivered via courier, and only take a small commission on it.

Tessa was doodling on the inside cover of her planner when I sat down in the chair next to her. She stopped immediately.

"Hi, Kate," she said. "How was your summer? How's Pankhurst?"

I told her I'd been in Italy, and she nodded, as if Italy was the most fascinating place she'd ever heard of. I didn't give her any details. I'd learned being guarded was a way to keep people interested.

"How about you?" I asked, out of politeness.

She told me about her belly-button piercing, and untucked her shirt to show me.

"That's a real diamond," Tessa said, tugging at it to give me what she thought was a better view even though our history teacher was coming round with sheets on Stalinism. "Just got to keep it covered for a while as it heals. I don't want anyone seeing it and making me take it out."

"Watch out for Ms Calding then," I said.

"Oh, yeah, her," said Tessa. "She reminds me of someone... I think from a Netflix series. Probably at that party my dad got me a VIP pass for in—"

65

"She reminds me of a weasel or a ferret," I interjected. Tessa's name-dropping got out of control if she wasn't stopped in time. "I miss Wibbz."

"The Wibbster was a legend," said Tessa. Even people who weren't in Pankhurst knew Wibbz because she had taught food tech classes, and everyone knew the anecdotes. "Remember when that girl in your house found the bone on the beach and Wibbz phoned the police and said a human leg had washed up, and it turned out to be from a cow?"

"That was a classic," I said. "She said there were no cows near Mount Norton and she was sure it was human and the police were covering something up." I thought of old Wibbz with her feet up on a chair, an ice-pack over each one, and a glass of wine by her side – or gin if it was the weekend – singing old campfire songs from her days as a guide leader.

As the class was told to pick up the first photocopied sheet, Tess whispered to me, "Made any plans for the Pankhurst party? Your house is first up, right? Where are you thinking of having it?"

"I have a mind-blowing spot in mind," I said.

Tessa's mouth made an "O" shape. "Where?"

I give her a regretful look. "I can't say yet."

"You'll definitely invite me, won't you?" she said. "I'm your history partner."

I tilted my head slightly. "We're partners because of a seating plan."

"Yeah, but ... please?"

I nodded, and she gave a gratifying little squeal.

In art, we chose our tables for the year. We each had one to ourselves. I picked the one nearest to the cabinet in which my ceramic dragons resided. Bernard, who was also in my class, took the table behind me. It was unavoidable as the class was small and he got to it first.

The term's topic was the human form. Bernard threw a small scrunched-up piece of paper at my head as I was attempting to draw my own hand. It ricocheted off and landed on my desk. I chucked it over my shoulder without looking at it.

"Want to see what I've done?" he called.

I swivelled round and sighed. This was bound to be predictable. "A nude?"

"Got it in one. It's you." He turned his sketchbook towards me. On the page was a figure that did look a little like me. I placed my hand over it. "Get rid of it."

Bernard was biting down on his pencil, grinning. "I've got an idea. I'll change it." He took the pencil and drew a Chinese-looking symbol tattoo on the leg and added a moustache. "Hang on," he said, and squiggled in some long ringletty curls. "There. Adorable."

I gave him what I hoped was a pitying look, and turned back to the picture of my hand, which looked amateur now I saw it afresh.

*

At the end of the day, I walked back with Meribel and Lo – we took the long route to confuse a couple of first-formers behind us. They meekly followed. We agreed it wasn't cruel – we were giving them more exercise.

Fruit and home-made cookies were waiting for us in the dining room. Squirrel told me I had post, and although I knew who it would be from, I went racing back into the hall to the pigeonholes and picked up the yellow envelope with the typed address label. My mother had an account with an online card company that sent me a card at the start of every term. I tucked my finger under the flap and pulled it open. On the front there was a cartoon penguin holding up a banner saying *Happy New Term, Kate!* Inside the message was *All the best, darling, Mama.*

I'd had the same card and the same message last term. Had she picked it out again or had the card company made an error? I put it back inside the envelope and buried it in the recycling bin, then told Meribel and Lo it was just junk mail when I returned to the dining room.

"Let's go to the other common room," said Meribel. "We'll hang out there for a bit before doing any homework. Maybe even" – she tilted her head with faux-mischievousness – "sit on the corner sofa. Can't have Clemmie thinking it's hers."

There were only two other people in Davison common room – sixth-form girls. They were at one of the tables in deep discussion, and glared at us when we ran towards the corner sofa, laughing. But just before we reached it,

Lo stopped and said, "What's happened to Veronica's collage?"

A piece of green paper had been attached with a drawing pin to the red silk in the middle of the artwork. It was a prescription. Lo reached it first.

"It's Zeta's," she said. "Why would someone have put it there?"

"Like it's a noticeboard," said Meribel.

I stood behind them. I sounded out the name of the medicine in my head. It was like a character in a sci-fi movie.

The door to the common room opened and a crowd of people streamed in, as if an event we hadn't known about had finished. Clemmie's voice was a dramatic cry. "Who put that on Vee's collage?"

"It was up there when we came in," Lo said.

"Really?" said Clemmie as if she didn't believe us. She prised off the drawing pin and took down the prescription. She held it up. "Someone's taking the piss out of your artwork, Vee."

Oh, my God, Veronica was here. I stepped back to let her through, and disassociate myself from this disaster. There was a small rip in the red silk where the drawing pin had been stuck in – surely Clemmie could have removed it more carefully? The room went silent.

Veronica touched the hole in the fabric that the drawing pin had made and frowned. "Anyone know who did this?"

There was a faint ripple of "no"s.

"Maybe Zeta dropped it, and a cleaner put it up there by mistake?" I said. I scanned the crowd for Zeta. Fortunately she wasn't there.

"A cleaner wouldn't do that. It's obviously artwork," said Veronica's friend Flo. "I mean there's a little sign next to it."

"What's the prescription for?" asked Paige.

Hugo took it from Clemmie, and read it out loud. "Look it up on your phone."

Someone laughed, and mentioned acne treatment. There was more laughter.

Monro snatched the paper from Hugo, and said, "That's not fair." He folded it in half and said, "This needs to go back to her." He handed it to me. "You take it."

I was flattered he'd trusted me, but then he added. "You're House Prefect, aren't you?" and I guessed that was why he'd given it to me. I placed it in the pocket of my school skirt.

"What about your artwork, Vee?" said Flo. "It's so disrespectful that someone would have done this."

Veronica shrugged. I admired that shrug. "It's not the end of the world," she said.

"I guess you've already got the prize money," said Monro. There was a shocked silence at this.

"Monro," said Hugo in a jokey voice. "Your empathy levels are dangerously low."

"Says the person who told Clemmie to look up the name of the medication," said Monro. He looked at the artwork. "Hopefully no real damage done, Vee?"

Veronica shook her head. "I'll get over it. Anyone want a game of pool? Flo?"

Everyone dispersed to various corners of the room and Meribel, Lo and I got to the corner sofa before Clemmie's crowd could. Lo had discovered a new band for us to stalk. I kept my eye on Hugo. He sat on his own at a table with his legs stretched out to the side, calling out to Clemmie to make him a cup of tea. I thought about going to talk to him about my party, just as an excuse; it wasn't often there was a spare seat next to him.

Too late. Clemmie's crowd invaded his space, gathering round the table with their mugs of tea, telling him loudly the prescription was for anxiety meds, and that totally figured. Most of us pretended we hadn't heard. Paige whispered something to them all, probably some story about Zeta.

Meribel played an excerpt of music out loud and people turned to give her a look and shame her into muting it. She lowered the volume slightly. Monro walked past Hugo's table and tripped over his legs. Hugo called him a clumsy bastard, and as he moved his legs under the table, he caught my eye. *What an idiot*, he said with his facial expression and I rolled my eyes in sympathy while my stomach flipped with delight. I was on Hugo's radar. He was sitting with Clemmie but he'd rather be with me.

CHAPTER 8

I handed the prescription to Calding since she was in the hall when we came back into Pankhurst, telling her someone had found it in Davison. I couldn't be bothered to involve myself any more than that. There was a low buzz at dinner among people who'd heard about it being pinned to Veronica's artwork. Zeta seemed oblivious until Calding asked to speak to her after dinner. I couldn't bear to see her panic as she wondered what it was about, so I repositioned my chair in order not to have her in my line of vision.

"Should we tell her?" asked Lo. I knew she felt more solidarity with Zeta because they were both scholarship girls. "She's started jiggling about now."

I turned. Clemmie was nudging other people to watch. I sighed heavily, and stood up. As a pretext, I took my glass to refill with water.

"Your prescription got handed in to Calding," I told her. "That's all she wants to see you about."

Zeta looked relieved, and didn't ask me how I knew. I could have finished the conversation at that point, but I was curious. "It was pinned to Veronica's artwork in Davison. D'you know how it could have ended up there?"

I saw incomprehension in Zeta's eyes as she shook her head. "I've never been to Davison," she said. "I knew I'd left it somewhere but I couldn't remember where."

"At least it wasn't lost," I said, and flashed a brief smile before going on to the water dispenser.

In my room afterwards, lying on my bed, looking up at the fairy lights I'd just hung up, Bel, Lo and I discussed who might have pinned the prescription to Veronica's collage. We agreed that the most likely contender was Clemmie. Davison common room would have been empty if she'd rushed back from school and gone straight there. She'd never minded about offending anyone or making them feel uncomfortable, even her friends – even Veronica.

We went on to dissect the day. I told them my new timetable was crap because I didn't have any lessons with Hugo, but three with Bernard. I described the moment I realized Bernard had drawn me nude. They laughed, and said I should report him for being inappropriate. I pointed out that I'd be filing reports 24/7 if I reported every piece of inappropriate behaviour at Mount Norton.

Meribel told us the new maths teacher had signed her whole class up for an inter-school maths competition the following month.

"Can you imagine anything more tragic?" she moaned.

Lo admitted she'd got seventy per cent in a biology test sprung on her that afternoon, and she was really annoyed she didn't get higher.

As we tried to give her the talk on her overly high expectations, she held up her hand to bat us away. "In other news," she said quietly. "I had this feeling all day about Sasha. As if I let her down."

"You didn't," I said quickly. I couldn't bear this. I thought it was over.

"Of course you didn't," said Meribel. "She let herself down."

Lo flicked the remote-control switch on my fairy lights and they turned green. It was the opposite of calming. "I should have listened to her side of the story, or at least got in contact as soon as I'd heard she'd been expelled."

"Her side of the story was she needed the scholarship. We know that," said Meribel. "It doesn't excuse her."

"I've looked for her on social media to see how she's doing," said Lo. "She's unfollowed me on everything and locked her accounts."

I breathed out. That was good.

"I know it's hard, but you have to move on," said Meribel. "Your ex-girlfriend wasn't the person you thought she was." She lifted her leg up and rotated it while holding her stomach. "I used to be able to do this without it hurting." She tried the other leg and gave up. "Let's do running club tonight. Lo, you can leave Pankhurst with a clear conscience because it's allowed. You need the fresh air. No excuses, either of you." She dragged Lo, then me off the bed and told us to get changed.

Running club was the best. It gave us a legitimate excuse to be out of Pankhurst on a Monday evening. Enough people usually turned up that the sports teacher in charge generally didn't notice if anyone peeled off from the route as long as the right amount of people returned at the allotted time. Running club wasn't about speed or personal bests – there was athletics club for that.

While I put on my running gear, I received the text I'd been waiting for from my godfather Steve. *Beach house dates confirmed. Get ready to PARTY!*

I cheered out loud – it was utterly brilliant timing. I'd take the other two up there this evening and tell them the news. Once Lo saw the venue, she wouldn't be able to resist: she'd risk the scholarship to be at the party. She loved that house even more than I did.

Running club met in the car park at the top of the cliff, where everyone flexed their trainers and fluorescent yellow bibs were handed out, as if we were on an outing from the local nursery school. It was open to everyone from all boarding houses, but there tended to be the same faces. It was mostly the younger years who came, but Veronica was there for the first time with Monro. They'd arrived before us, and Monro was doing elaborate stretches, black neoprene braces on both knees, as if he was a hardcore runner. Lo made a *who-does-he-think-he-is?* face.

We ran at the back of the group, then hung back and ducked behind the first lot of thick gorse bushes where we removed the fluorescent bibs, and watched the others carry on, bobbing along like a dotted highlighter line.

"You know what I'm craving?" said Lo once we'd shoved the bibs into the small backpack I'd brought along for the purpose, so we didn't have well-meaning members of the public telling us our group had gone on ahead. "Chips from the beach café. With extra vinegar." She stood up and said, "Let's go."

The café would be closing up. Kipper, the guy who worked there, was temperamental and it would depend on his mood. We doubled back along the cliff at a brisk walking pace, and ran down the zigzag path.

When we reached the café, the open sign was still up. An older couple was coming out, bringing the smell of frying with them. Lo caught the door and went in first. Kipper – we'd never heard anyone use his real name – was still in his apron. He was in his late twenties or thirties and in the third form we used to think he was quite fit for his age. Now we agreed he used too much product in his hair, was definitely dodgy and he needed to work on his customer service skills.

"Café's closed," he said.

"Noooo," said Lo. "You're joking." If it had been Meribel who was desperate for chips, the wail would have been a lot louder.

"I'm cleaning up," said Kipper. "You're too late, angel, unless you've come about a part-time job."

"Nope, just chips," said Lo.

"You've still got the open sign on the door," said Meribel. She was looking at the strange ornaments made from imported shells on the shop side of the café. Some had been made into dogs, others into little people.

"I haven't had time to turn over the sign yet," said Kipper. "Don't pick up anything you're not intending to buy."

"Well, apparently I can't buy it because you're closed," said Meribel. I wished she hadn't. It made her sound snotty, playing into the stereotype of how the villagers saw us Nortonians, and he knew which school we were from because we'd been down here in our uniforms plenty of times.

I waited for Kipper to tell us to get out, but instead he smiled. He had very white teeth. We'd discussed them once and decided they were veneers, picturing his stumpy pared-down teeth before the veneers were fitted.

"I know some of your lot had a party here, on the roof," Kipper said. "I'd like you to pass the word round: I won't tolerate another one. The place was left in a hell of a mess."

I could tell from the others' faces that they were as panicked as I felt.

"Don't get me wrong," said Kipper, losing some of his aggressive tone. "I don't mind you enjoying yourselves. I'm all for that. Just not here." He picked up a dirty cloth. "Right, get lost. I've got cleaning up to do."

We couldn't reach the door fast enough.

Outside, we laughed. "He's so creepy," gasped Meribel. "Imagine getting a job with him. You'd have to be desperate."

"Forget Kipper, I've got something to show you two," I said. I led the way along the promenade towards the steps. "We need to go back up on the cliff path."

Meribel groaned. "Really? I bet there's time to go to the chip shop in Norton village if we pick up the pace. I'm starting to fancy them now too."

"It'll be worth it. I promise," I said. "Follow me."

The party would be exceptional. I was Kate Lynette Jordan-Ferreira. I wouldn't let Pankhurst down.

CHAPTER 9

Lo and Meribel were stunned when I said the beach house was booked for the first party of the season. They agreed every aspect of it was perfect. Not just the brilliant location – with the view, the seclusion and easy walking distance to all boarding houses – the house itself was beautiful. Lo said nothing would stop her being there.

Meribel nodded vigorously. "It's house tradition. Sneller might give you a one-day suspension, if she's forced to. Don't worry about Calding – it's what Sneller says that counts."

Lo hugged my arm. "Kate, you're going to raise the party bar so high this year nobody will be able to match it."

"It's going to be the day of the Autumn party," I said.

Meribel said, "Whoa! That's less than three weeks."

"That's plenty of time," I said with more confidence than I felt. My parents were always throwing parties in Dubai, but they used event planners and caterers.

The house looked unoccupied, but a window cleaner appeared from down the side of the house to ask what we were doing when we stepped over the low fence into the garden to take photos.

"Nothing," I said before anyone mentioned we had a booking. "It's just a really nice house. We've watched it be rebuilt."

"You should see inside," said the man. "Gorgeous. You wouldn't believe how much it costs to rent. Lucky for some, huh?"

We rejoined the back of the fluorescent running snake by waiting behind the gorse bushes and stepping out carefully, so our clothes didn't snag on the prickles. Veronica and Monro were last.

As they slow-jogged past us, Monro said, "Oh, now I get it. Running club is just a cover for some people."

"How did you get to the sixth form and not work that out?" I said. The three of us were walking quickly, and were managing to keep up with them pretty well. "Are you even a Mount Nortonian?"

"Call me stupid, but I genuinely thought people went running in running clubs," said Monro.

"I'm the slowest runner in the world," said Veronica. "Let's walk for a bit, M." She breathed out as if she was blowing out a candle. "I'm not doing this again."

"You didn't have to come with me," said Monro. "In fact I remember suggesting you didn't."

The three of us glanced at each other to signal our slight amusement at their bickering.

"You want to know where we've been?" said Meribel. She looked at me and I gave her a nod. She understood as well as I did that we needed the right people to get behind the party. Veronica might be annoyed my venue was better than her rooftop one, but I hoped she'd want the next Pankhurst party to be a success too.

I watched her face break into a wide smile when Meribel told her about the beach house. I was embarrassed how much I cared what she thought.

"It's lucky I have a godfather to help out," I said.

"Even so," said Veronica. "Nice work, Miss Jordan-Ferreira."

I beamed.

"You pulling off that location will rattle Hugo," said Monro. "When's it Churchill's turn?"

"Churchill's sixth." As House Prefect, I knew the rota exactly.

Lo relayed what Kipper had said about the beach café party, and Veronica grimaced. "I didn't think we'd left it in too bad a state."

"Kipper freaks me out," said Meribel. She gave a dramatic shudder.

"I saw him give Clemmie his phone number once," said Veronica. "Can you imagine?"

We winced.

"Kipper and Clemmie?" said Monro. "No. I can't imagine that." At the car park, we spread out and were taken through some cursory cool-down exercises. I noticed Monro spent more time retying his laces than doing any stretches. It was a shame Hugo wasn't here. The lunging would have been much more fun.

Next to me Meribel was actually talking about Hugo. "He's top of the guest list, right?"

I nodded. "Yep."

Meribel rattled off other names in our year and the sixth form. There were certain people we had to invite. Clemmie was a given. To not invite her would make people have to choose between us, and I couldn't risk that.

"Zeta?" suggested Lo, leaning in as she we stretched our sides.

"Nope," I said. "Sorry." I couldn't afford to be soft. It was for A-listers only.

"Bernard, I suppose," said Meribel.

I nodded. He was somehow attached to the Sussex clique through somebody's cousin, so it was kind of expected. "Sure," I said.

As we were dismissed from the car park to walk back to

our boarding houses, Veronica said, "If you want any tips on how to organize the party, let me know."

"Thanks." I walked next to them, and as we passed Monro's car, he gave it a pat.

"You've got to move that somewhere less obvious soon," said Veronica. "Lots of teachers walk this way and they'll see you with it."

"School rules about cars are pathetic," said Monro. "You should run one of your campaigns."

"Sorry, Monro, I don't feel strongly enough about the issue," retorted Veronica. "In fact I have some environmental concerns about it."

Meribel and Lo were walking faster, and had gone ahead. I didn't know whether to catch them up, but Veronica asked whether I was still making dragon sculptures, and I became so engrossed in telling her about the problems of the early models exploding in the kiln that we were suddenly at Davison, where she said goodbye and turned off. The other two had almost reached Pankhurst. I couldn't leave Monro on his own and run to catch them up, so the two of us walked together for a few minutes. My mind was on the party. It was so much more of a reality now.

He broke the silence between us. "Why dragons?"

Because they're strong and fiery, was the first thing that came into my mind. "I don't know," I said.

"Satisfying shapes?" suggested Monro.

I nodded. "I like doing the wings." I sounded dull,

dull, dull. Why did I care? It didn't matter. It was only Monro. The other two were going up the steps to Pankhurst's front door now, and Meribel stopped to wave at me. I waved back to indicate I'd seen they were going inside, but then she did an unsubtle pointy finger at Hugo, who was standing outside Churchill, on the other side of Pankhurst. He was leaning against the brick wall, on his phone making an actual call.

From the way he was waving his free hand around, it looked like a heavy conversation.

"I must tell Hugo about the party," I said to Monro. "You go on, I'll wait for him."

"Sure," said Monro.

"I hope you can make it too," I added. "It'll be the night of the Autumn Party."

He hesitated.

"There's nothing else happening that night, is there?" I pressed him.

"Nope. Nothing other than practising polite conversation in the assembly hall, which is always such a joy," said Monro. "Bye then."

"Bye." I waited by the Pankhurst steps as he walked on. He went past Hugo, raising his arm in a slight greeting gesture, but Hugo was intent on his phone call. "I've got to go, Janetta," he said. "And I'm blocking you now."

Ah, Janetta, the ex-girlfriend. Now blocked and completely out of the way.

He hung up. "Hi, Kate," he called. He shoved his

phone in the pocket of his rugby club hoodie. "You waiting for me?"

I gave a vague gesture which I hoped implied I'd only waited a brief moment, and I hadn't in any way been eavesdropping on his conversation. "I just thought I'd tell you about the Pankhurst party. We have a date and venue."

He nodded. "Well done. And?"

I told him, waiting for his reaction about the venue. There was a flicker of something, but all he said was, "I'll keep that date free."

It nearly fell out of my mouth that I already knew he was free because it was the evening of the compulsory-to-attend Autumn Party, but I said, "Great."

"I'll help you with the guest list," he said. He came closer and I loved how he could look so attractive in simple trackies and a hoodie.

"It's OK," I said. "I can always ask Veronica if I need to."

Hugo nodded. "I love Vee to bits, but she doesn't always understand how things should be done." He looked apologetic. "That's just between the two of us. I reckon you and I are on the same wavelength. Don't you think?"

I nodded. I wanted very much to be on the same wavelength as him.

CHAPTER 10

I forgot to put my phone on silent and woke abruptly to a WhatsApp from Elsie Gran telling me she was off to water the allotment. It was 5.25 a.m. I flicked through my parents' social media accounts. They were at some kind of trade fair for their plastic surgery business. Their stand was impressive. It had all the promise of a smart reception desk at a spa: clean, white and expensive, with a stunning floral arrangement. To one side was a board of photos, showing before and afters. There were several photos of beautiful people standing next to my father. Often clients didn't like to be seen with their plastic surgeon, so he'd have been happy about that.

A notification came through on my phone: Elsie Gran had sent me an image. It was a blurred selfie of her in her charity shop sweatshirt and leggings perched on the raised wall of one of her allotment beds, looking intently at the wrong bit of the phone. I saw she had a cigarette tucked behind her hand. She didn't think I'd enlarge the photo and see it. She looked surprisingly sweet. It made me want to wrap my arms around her.

A party to-do list, that's what I needed to do. I typed as much as I could think of into a Notes page before feeling overwhelmed, then I got out of bed to take a photo of the sky for Elsie Gran. It was pale pink, and the sea was flat like shiny glass. I stepped out on to the fire escape in my T-shirt nightie, the smooth metal under my bare feet comfortingly warm. I took a photo and sent it, then put my phone down on the window sill. It felt as if nobody else was up. I couldn't even hear Squirrel crashing about in the kitchens. There was no traffic, just the swish of trees outside Churchill moving in the sea breeze, the bird calls, and the gentle flap of my curtains against the window frame. I stood on one leg, closed my eyes, and breathed in and out, imagining I was at a yoga class.

On opening my eyes, I lost balance and fell against the railing, and as I looked across to Churchill I locked eyes with Monro. He was sitting with his legs up on the bench drinking a mug of tea or coffee, dressed in shorts and a T-shirt. He looked as startled as me but recovered first to give a small wave. He said something which I couldn't hear so I leaned forward, cupping my hand to my ear.

He swivelled his legs off the bench, and came closer to the fence, and I leaned over the railing so it dug into my stomach. "Come over," he said. It was half a question. He held his mug up. "Tea?"

Company is exactly what I needed. I nodded and glanced down at my long T-shirt. I'd put on some underwear and some other clothes first, obviously.

Monro placed the mug on the arm of the bench, and held up his hands four times to tell me the code for Churchill's back gate.

After changing, I sent a quick message to Lo and Bel in case they came into my room and found me gone. It was unlikely they'd worry and alert Calding, but better to be safe than sorry.

It was strange to be sneaking out at this time of day – at least in the daylight I could see exactly where I was going. I'd been in Churchill a few times to play tennis – entering via the main entrance. I'd never used the back gate.

Lo once told me Clemmie said Lo and the other Pankhurst scholarship students had to do a challenge when they were all in the first form to prove they had what it took to be "full members of the school". Lo, Zeta and Sasha were told to run round the perimeter of the Churchill grounds on their own at night. They did it because they thought it would be a laugh. Clemmie had let them in through the back gate herself, after presumably buying the code. What Lo, Zeta and Sasha didn't know was that running there would set off a series of security lights and a furious, barking housemaster's dog. When they ran back to the gate, Clemmie had gone and they didn't know the code to get out. They were returned to Wibbz by the livid housemaster.

Monro had managed to make tea in the time it had taken me to pull on more clothing and come over.

"What are you doing up so early?" I asked, as he handed me the mug that was waiting for me on the arm of the bench. "Thanks."

"Same as you," he said, settling back down where he'd been sitting earlier.

"But it might not be the same reason as me," I said. I sat next to him; it felt as if we were at an allotment social. "I just woke up early."

"Me too," he said. I saw the scar on his arm from when he put it through a window in Churchill and resisted a bizarre compulsion to touch it. It had been pretty dramatic, according to various accounts. Masses of blood and lots of shouting. I hadn't been at Mount Norton at the time.

There were things I wanted to ask him – what people thought of Clemmie back in Sussex, what was going on between him and Veronica, and about his anger issues – but I didn't dare, and remarked instead, "It's nice without everyone up."

He nodded, and I sipped my tea.

"It doesn't feel quite so much like a prison at this time of the day," he said.

"You hate school that much?" I asked.

He made a face. "It's complicated." He shifted on the bench and winced. "My leg hurts a bit after that run," he said. "Pathetic, isn't it?"

"You have to build it up," I said. "Meribel and Lo hate running, but I quite like it, and it gets better the more you do it. Sometimes it feels like I'm bounding along like a dog and nothing hurts." I put my mug down beside me and mimed ears flapping in the breeze with my hands either side of my head, before I imagined how foolish I looked, and picked up my mug again.

He smiled politely. "I wanted to ask you something," he said, and I felt it: the shift in conversation to something of weight.

"I heard a rumour," he said, "that Sasha Mires's expulsion was something to do with Clemmie."

That was definitely not what I was expecting. "Really? Who's been spreading that?" Sweat prickled at the back of my neck.

Monro hesitated. "Veronica told me."

I pulled myself together. What he'd told me was a way in to ask about Clemmie or Veronica, and I chose Veronica first. "Are you two in a thing?"

"You think me and Veronica. . ." He pulled a surprised face. "Really? No, we're close, but we're just mates."

"Right." I thought about this. "You're on her artwork though. Why's it called *The Things We Keep Hidden*? What's the hidden thing?"

He looked away. "That's just her being cryptic. It's because we know so much about each other. We've known each other all our lives."

"So why did Veronica say that about Sasha's explusion?" I asked.

"Clemmie's mum told Vee's mum they'd been sent a letter from Sasha's dad."

"What?" There was a trickle of sweat like a raindrop down a windowpane travelling down my neck. I'd seen Sasha's parents at school events. They were quiet and ordinary-looking. I remembered her father was much taller than her mother. He'd had a beard.

"How did he get her address?" I asked. "What did it say?" I moved a little closer.

Monro lifted a shoulder. "I don't know how he got the address. The letter said he and his wife wanted to establish the facts around their daughter's expulsion, and they had reason to believe Clemmie was involved."

"What did Clemmie's parents do?" I asked softly.

"Got a lawyer to fire off a letter saying they'd sue for false accusations and harassment."

I waited for him to add more detail, but he didn't. "You know you're spreading the rumour by telling me," I said.

The corners of Monro's mouth twitched downwards in acknowledgement. "True, but I thought you might know something."

"Why would I know anything?"

"You were with Clemmie that night, weren't you? That's what I heard."

I really wanted to rub the back of my neck to stop the prickling sensation, but I forced myself not to. "We were working on our geography project," I said. "She came to our room, mine and Lo's. I wasn't really aware of the time, but she was there from soon after dinner to just before Lo came back from dance club."

It was my go-to statement. Each time I said it, it came out more wooden than the time before.

"I didn't think you two were friends," said Monro.

"We're not," I said. "We'd been paired up for geography." I paused. "I know she's part of your crowd, but I can't stand her."

Monro chucked the last dregs of tea out of his mug and on to the grass. "She's not too fond of you either."

CHAPTER 11

At breakfast I filled Meribel and Lo in on my early morning encounter with Monro, although I left out the conversation about Clemmie. They weren't as interested as I thought they'd be; they couldn't get past the idea that I'd got up so early.

Before we'd finished eating, Calding stood up and clapped her hands for silence. She announced there'd been a spot check in our rooms for contraband items while we'd been in the dining hall. There was a collective intake of breath at this – in the past, searches had never happened in the first week of term. We hadn't even noticed Calding and the Ghost had left the dining hall. They'd worked unbelievably fast.

As Calding read out a shortlist of girls she wanted to see after she'd finished speaking, I accidentally caught Lo's eye. This is what had happened the day Sasha had left and never come back. Hers had been one of the names read out by Wibbz at breakfast.

We had assumed Sasha's vodka had been found in the room she shared with Clemmie. She hadn't had much at all, just a little which she'd kept in a perfume bottle. We thought Wibbz had conducted the best search of her life, going round sniffing perfume bottles. Nobody was worried about major repercussions.

Later, we learned a scholarship paper due to be set in the coming weeks had been found under Sasha's mattress. It was a maths and science exam. She was suspended, and her parents came to pick her up the same day. The suspension turned into an expulsion. They worked out that a deputy head had left his laptop in Wibbz's unlocked office while he dropped by for a board game evening in the junior common room a week earlier, and that was the only time the paper could have been printed off.

Sasha had been at the board game evening but left early because she said she had revision to do.

I provided an alibi for Clemmie, and everybody else in Pankhurst was either at the board game evening or somewhere else where another person could vouch for them.

This morning four girls had their names read out. Two of them were first-formers and they were already in tears.

Clemmie carried on eating her cereal, tipping her bowl to scoop up the last few spoonfuls.

In art I told Bernard about the beach house party, and sat back as he made the right responses: a mini whoop of admiration followed by curiosity as to how I managed to secure the venue.

"Cool godfather," he breathed.

He stayed at my desk, as I copied a pudgy toddler hand from a photo, telling Mr Hayes, the art teacher, that he was sketching my eyes. "You've got to stare into my eyes now," he told me when Mr Hayes had gone past.

"Sorry, I don't have time," I said.

"All right. Let's talk guests," Bernard said, undaunted, as he drew some generic eyes on a piece of watercolour paper that he'd taken from my art folder. "I wouldn't bother inviting Monro. He'll only injure himself, or spread bad vibes."

I stopped shading in a fingernail on my sketch. "What is it with you two?" I asked.

Bernard made a face as if to say *Isn't it obvious?* "He's unpredictable. There's something not right about him. He picked a fight with me in the first form and was nearly expelled for it." He leaned forward and said, "Keep away from him." He pulled back and said, "He'll be one of those guys who goes berserk, and I'll be the only one who saw it coming."

"Monro? You're joking."

Bernard shook his head. "Nope. Mount Norton is full of nutters. Dunno why it attracts them." He touched me lightly on the arm. "You and me, though. We're sound."

I moved on to the next fingernail and began shading again.

"Of course, you probably feel you *have* to invite him, with Veronica being part of his crowd, and her being at Pankhurst. I get that." Bernard quickly added a few eyelashes to the one lone eye he'd drawn, and folded his arms on top of it. "So how can I help with the party? You want me to find bouncers? I'll get a couple of guys from the rugby club for you. What about a playlist?"

Meribel's new phone was waiting for her in her pigeonhole when we returned from school. Calding came out of her office when she heard us.

"You three. I'd like to discuss your roles as House Prefect and deputies. Please would you give me a few moments of your time?" She ushered us in.

We trooped into her office, rolling our eyes at each other. There was no trace of the comfortable, padded chairs Wibbz used to have in her office. Instead, we had to take a hard plastic one from the stack by the wall.

We let Calding do the talking. She started off saying, "I'm concerned your roles aren't balanced enough." We nodded attentively as she spoke, knowing we'd fight her all the way if she did what she was threatening to, which was give us responsibility for lower school prep, and take on some night-time chores, such as ensuring lights were switched off. I could see the appeal of having more power over the younger girls, but for what? Frankly I had better things to do with my time.

As Calding spoke I looked round the office. She had managed to de-personalise it in quite a spectacular way. When Wibbz occupied it, there'd been piles of papers everywhere, and loads of photographs on her desk of her two round-faced, smiley nephews as children. They had turned into flabby-cheeked jovial men by the time they appeared in a family wedding shot which used to hang above the filing cabinet.

The filing cabinet was rumoured to be full to the top with Wibbz's snacks. There'd been a boarding house challenge set soon after I arrived, by the then House Prefect, to get a photo of the inside of it, but it had always been locked. It remained an open challenge, like taking a selfie wearing the peculiar hairnet that Squirrel wore when she served food.

Wibbz had had a "Pankhurst wall" where she taped photos of Pankhurst alumni – in graduation gowns, hard hats on building sites, several with musical instruments, in fabulous outfits at gallery openings, girls in costume on stage, and in pride of place the girl who'd got a role in *Emmerdale*, Wibbz's favourite soap.

All that had gone. Calding had nothing on the walls except a noticeboard. On it was a single sheet of emergency numbers, a drawing pin in each corner. It was more like a resources room now, with a paper shredder, laminator, paper trimmer and new printer on the shelves where Wibbz's celebrity magazines had been stacked.

Calding had come to the end of her thoughts.

"I can't speak for the others," I said. I was Kate Lynette Jordan-Ferreira. I had made myself a somebody in this school. "Personally, I'd like to think over what you've said. I don't want to rush into anything."

She wasn't expecting me to treat her as a colleague. She blinked. Frustration. Disdain for my arrogance, maybe. It was so obvious she wasn't used to a school like Mount Norton. Meribel and Lo murmured they felt exactly the same.

"Is that all?" I asked.

"Yes," said Calding stiffly.

We kept our bubbling-up laughter inside until we were in the dining hall, spluttering over tea and flapjacks. We wrapped up extra flapjacks in a napkin to take to Davison.

Walking into the common room, we found a commotion inside. People were crowded round Veronica's artwork. Veronica herself was taking a photo of it. Attached was an article. Lo read the headline as we grew closer. *"Teenager's unusual hobby."* It was about Flo. She was dressed in armour of some description. A few people stepped away as I leaned in to read the article. Flo was a fan of historical re-enactments.

Flo said angrily, "OK, folks. Show's over. Anyone want to confess to stalking me on the internet and going to the trouble of printing this out and ruining Vee's artwork?" She turned to Veronica. "Got enough evidence?"

Veronica stopped photographing. "Yes, you can take it down now."

Bernard said, "Who thinks armour is a sexy look?"

"Not me," said Hugo.

"Shut up," said Veronica. "I don't know why Flo's kept it a secret because it's pretty cool."

"It's creepy that someone would do this," said Flo.

"*Historical role-play* is creepy," said Paige.

Monro was sitting at a table with a laptop, away from everyone, taking no interest in the discussion. I thought he'd at least look up to acknowledge my presence but he must have been too engrossed in what he was doing.

"The artwork looks strangely empty now," said another of Veronica's friends. I knew what she meant. The photo of Veronica and Monro in the corner looked even smaller.

Hugo said, "Put your artwork in a massive box frame. That will stop it being used as a noticeboard."

"Someone thinks they're being clever – if you hadn't given it that title, this might not have happened," said Clemmie.

"Interesting," said Veronica. "You're saying it's my own fault?"

"Course not," said Clemmie. "Stop being so sensitive."

I was intrigued. The two of them weren't usually snappy with each other.

"It won't look good in a box frame," said Veronica. She smoothed a piece of orange felt at the corner, as if it might be coming unstuck. "Maybe I should let it be interactive. Go ahead and use it, folks. Keep it anonymous, though. No more naming and shaming."

"But it's literally prize-winning art," said Flo.

"I don't care, not really," said Veronica, stepping back and tilting her head. She straightened the frame. "As Monro pointed out yesterday, I've already got the prize money."

"It's not like you even need the money," said Clemmie.

Veronica gave her a stare, and Clemmie turned away first.

Veronica went to join Monro at his table. I noticed he didn't make any move to hide what was on his laptop screen from her, but when Bernard, walking by on his way to the pool table, darted towards Monro to press a random key on the keyboard to annoy him, Monro snapped the lid shut, narrowly missing Bernard's hand. Then he jumped up and went up close to Bernard's face, yelling at him to keep away.

"Calm down," said Bernard. "You need to watch that temper of yours."

CHAPTER 12

I woke early again a couple of days later, and when I pulled one of my curtains back, the pale-orange strip of the horizon almost matched curtain fabric. I lifted the window and stepped out. Immediately I went to the right-hand-side railings to see if Monro was there.

He was, and I wondered for a moment if he'd been on that bench the last two mornings waiting for me or if it was coincidence. He must have heard the window opening because he was looking up at me. I waved, and he made a drinking motion, though I noticed he didn't have a mug himself. Before I could answer, he moved an imaginary steering wheel, and pointed in the direction of the car park. He was suggesting a ride in his car.

I made an exaggeratedly surprised face in case anything more subtle was hard to read, then lifted my hands up in a why-not gesture, and went back inside to pile on a few clothes and toothbrush away my morning breath.

When I went through Pankhurst back gate, he was waiting.

"Where are we going?" I asked.

"Out for breakfast," he said, and held up a red thermos.

My parents would have loathed Monro's car, which came to life on the third try, and made a grinding noise as it started to move. It was even more decrepit than Elsie Gran's old Volvo. A faint smell of damp hung in the air, and it couldn't have still been the lingering aroma of Bel's wet trainers. I wound the window down (no electrics) and the smell dissipated a little.

I hardly knew anywhere around Mount Norton beyond the village of Norton, and Ryemouth where we went to shop if we didn't want to buy online. Monro said we were going to Thornley harbour, but I'd never heard of it.

Once we were on the main road, it was almost too noisy to talk, especially with the window down, so after a shouted conversation about how fast the car could go (allegedly quite fast when it was warmed up), I didn't bother. I let the wind mess my hair and take my breath away. The freedom of being away from Pankhurst and nobody knowing was exhilarating. And I was with the wild card who was Monro – which was just plain thrillingly weird.

"Here we are," he said, turning into what looked like a driveway between houses. Almost immediately I saw the sea, and a large empty car park and some green space where a few people were walking dogs. "There's a neat place across from the mouth of the harbour. You'll like it."

I kicked off my pale blue suede flip-flops and brought my knees up to the seat and clasped them. "This is so much nicer than the coast at Norton. Why haven't I been here before?"

"Because you only stick with Norton beach and Ryemouth?" suggested Monro as he parked up close to the water.

"Or maybe because there's no public transport here," I said primly. I hadn't seen a bus stop for a while.

A line of narrow yachts were attached to moorings, and there was a stretch of land the other side of a small channel of water at the harbour mouth. Across there was a collection of oversized beach huts, pastel colours gleaming in the early morning light, far superior to the small, murky green ones on Norton beach.

At the other end of the car park, two men were bent over fishing nets and baskets but otherwise there was nobody about. Two seagulls were fighting over something, and behind their squawks was the constant clanking from the yachts.

"I love that sound," I said.

"The halyards against the mast?" said Monro as he untangled himself from his seat belt. "D'you sail?"

"Not really," I said. I'd been on various yachts with my parents, but crew members had done everything.

"Sailing can be intense," he said. "If you do it with my dad. He's not the most patient of people."

Maybe the anger issues everyone talked about stemmed from his dad.

We left the car and walked towards the small quay, Monro holding the thermos. There was a closed café, boarded-up fish stall and a lifeboat station. A blackboard sign announced that the first ferry across to the headland would be at nine a.m.

"This way," said Monro, bounding down the steps next to the sign. He stepped on to the small boat at the bottom. It creaked. The name on the side had been freshly painted: *Tiger Lily*. "*Tiger Lily's* making a special early-morning crossing," he called to me. "Leaving in one minute."

I watched him scramble towards the back of the boat as I went down the steps. What time was Monro planning to get back to school?

"Are you allowed to start this?" I said, stepping cautiously on to it, and crouching down towards the wooden bench in the middle so I didn't wobble it too much.

Monro squatted next to the motor. "Very poor security. As long as we get it back here before the first official crossing at nine a.m., we'll be fine."

The motor roared suddenly, and *Tiger Lily* jolted, causing me to sit down abruptly. I let go of my doubts and laughed. It felt so ridiculous to be doing this on a school morning, with a boy I barely knew. Monro laughed too as he sat down, his laughter spilling out unexpectedly, as if it had been squashed into a small tin and the lid had flown open. If I looked out towards the sea and not directly at Monro, I could almost imagine he was Hugo, and we were off on a romantic getaway.

He turned the boat towards the headland before cutting the speed and his high spirits at the same time. "Life jackets. I didn't think about them." He searched with one hand under the bench where he was sitting, then quickly knelt to get a better look.

"I can swim." Had he never noticed me on Norton beach in the summer? I was an extremely competent swimmer.

Monro pulled out a life jacket. "This water has a current."

"I'll be OK," I said.

"Please," he said. "Put it on. There's only one and I want you to wear it."

It was damp and streaked with black grease. "Seriously?"

"Seriously. *Tiger Lily* is about to accelerate."

I struggled into it, adjusting the clips so it fitted me more snugly. The boat roared, and reared up so I had to hold on to the bench I was on. Cold, dirty-looking water swilled over my flip-flops, and I wriggled them off, holding them in one hand, and hung on to the side of the boat with the other.

Ahead was the beach-hut world, clean and fresh in the early sunshine, pastel-coloured calm.

The crossing only took a few minutes. I imagined it took a lot longer when *Tiger Lily* was a working ferry. There was a wooden jetty the other side, and Monro parked alongside expertly, cutting the engine and letting the boat drift towards a metal ring. He reached down for some rope and tied a loose knot through it, then scrambled on to the jetty to hold the boat steady for me to disembark.

I took off the life jacket, and left it with my flip-flops on the bench. It seemed like a barefoot kind of place.

"Follow me for the best breakfast spot," Monro said, and set off in the opposite direction to what I was expecting, towards the headland, the rocky part where I couldn't see the violence of the waves yet but I could hear it. It was OK for him, he was wearing Vans.

I looked back at my flip-flops in the boat.

"You'll be OK," said Monro. "I'll help you."

He didn't take my hand until we reached the first pile of boulders, and I slid on the first one and shrieked. I gripped with my toes after that, and we clambered towards the highest rock.

At the top there was a smooth, flat surface, a seat above the rage of the water. It was small though. We sat close together, thighs touching, my breathing different because of the gusty, salty air. I had a feeling of letting go, of not caring about the fine sea spray that shot up now and again

106

when a big wave hit the rocks below. I looked at the blurry white-blue line of the horizon, and thought how random it was that I was here instead of in bed. I was surprised he hadn't tried to take a selfie of the two of us yet. It sounded vain but there were a lot of boys at Mount Norton who wanted to be seen with me.

"What are you thinking about?" asked Monro. His hair was slightly flattened on one side where he must have slept on it. It was quite cute.

"Nothing much," I said. I watched him unscrew the lid of his thermos and pour tea into it. He offered it to me, and I took two sips before handing it back. "Thanks."

He drank from the other side of it and refilled it. "It has a metallic taste from being in here, but I quite like it." He handed it to me again and pulled a bar of fruit and nut chocolate from his pocket. It was bent out of shape, snapped in various places already.

He opened out the wrapper and laid it on the rock, and we ate it slowly.

"I know I sound like my grandad, but I love this view," said Monro, as he pulled a fat raisin out of his chunk of chocolate and chucked it into his mouth before eating the rest. "Not that my grandad has ever seen this view."

I acknowledged this by saying, "Hm."

"There are views that you know you're going to miss as soon you look at them." He turned to me. "Don't you think?"

107

I didn't know how to respond, but I said, "Have you been to this place a lot?"

He shook his head. "I came to the fish restaurant on the harbour with my parents one Saturday last year. Then I came here with Vee a couple of times – in a taxi. You should see how much Vee racks up on her taxi account for someone so interested in the environment. One time it was early, like now, before the ferry had started, and we came across on *Tiger Lily*."

"I feel bad for Veronica about her artwork," I said. "I wouldn't be taking it so well."

"No need to feel bad," he said.

I raised my eyes at him. "That's kind of brutal."

He crumpled the chocolate wrapper and rammed it into his pocket without looking at it. "It's not. Spoiler alert: she always planned for it to be interactive. She put Zeta's prescription and the article about Flo up there herself. It's part of her project."

"What? That's mad," I said. Was he spinning me a story here?

"I know. She said she thought the prescription was for eczema. She saw it in the pigeonholes in Pankhurst when she was walking past after dinner. Even so." Monro shook his head with what I took to be disapproval. "I wasn't going to out her, but she shouldn't have done it. She should have picked things that weren't going to embarrass people. Or blanked out their names."

"Why did she do it?" It didn't make any sense to me.

"It's the Things We Keep Hidden theme. She wanted to start it off and make it noticeable. It's a whole long project." He turned his hand over to show his palm in a don't-ask-me-why gesture. "It had the desired effect. People loved it, didn't they? Now she's waiting for other people to join in."

He left a pause, and I thought there might be more to the project than he was saying.

I picked up a small rock by my foot and threw it into the water. "Aren't you worried I'm going to tell everyone about Vee's artwork?" I said. It was the first time in my life I'd called her Vee out loud.

"Not really."

"You think I can keep quiet about something like that?"

"If you do tell, that's part of the interactive process." He brushed his palms together, and checked for chocolate crumbs. "How about keeping it quiet for a bit longer though?"

"Hmmm. I'll have to see."

We sat for a while, chucking rocks into the sea. We tried to skim the flatter ones so they'd bounce on the water before sinking, but we failed, and I said, "Let's go round to the beach huts." I clambered down far more easily than I had done going up.

We walked the length of the huts. They had porches, curtains and running water – I could tell by the drains. They were more like mobile homes than beach huts. A young couple jogged along in the sand.

I sighed. "It looks so nice." I'd like to have said that out of all the beaches I'd been to, and I'd been to a lot, this had to be one of my favourites. But it would have sounded over the top, so I didn't.

We walked back to *Tiger Lily* and Monro untied it deftly. Water hit our faces as we bumped back over the waves. There were more people around when we reached the other side. A woman with a little white dog gave us a double-look as Monro secured the boat to the post he'd taken it from. I held my hand out for him to help me haul myself up on to land, and when he almost fell backwards, he gripped me tightly and our slightly hysterical laughter filled the still, morning air. I had to look away from him after a couple of seconds, because I had a thought in my head that with the sun beginning to burn through the clouds and the clanking of the masts, and the salty taste on my lips, this would be the ideal place to kiss someone. I nearly leaned in towards Monro, to see what it would be like. The lightness was there in my body and the sensation of arching towards something. I knew I liked him a whole lot more after this trip, but I steadied myself. I didn't want to mess up my chances with Hugo.

I wondered if Monro would mind if I brought Hugo here sometime.

CHAPTER 13

It was 6.55 a.m. when I slipped in through Pankhurst's back gate. I thought I saw a shadowy face appear at a window, but when I looked again it was just the ripple effect of a curtain.

I climbed through my window and found Meribel lying on my bed, swiping through her phone.

"Out with Mad Monro?" she asked.

I threw my salt-water-damaged flip-flops on to the floor and lay next to her. "Yep, but don't call him that. We went to Thornley beach for breakfast. In his car."

She looked mildly impressed. "There was a café open?"

As soon as she heard the word thermos she was less impressed. "Bet he's quite the one for deep conversation. He knows he's in the friend zone, right? "

"Of course," I said.

"Keep him in the outer edge," continued Meribel.

"Really?"

"He's just odd, don't you think? Not odd as in creative. Odd as in odd."

I frowned. "He's not so odd when you get to know him."

Meribel waved her arms in the air. "Nooo! Get out while you can."

I laughed and said I needed a shower. She sat up and said I hadn't told her anything interesting yet, so she wasn't going to leave. I peeled off my top, and said, "Suit yourself, Bel."

I watched Calding stir two teaspoons of sugar into her black coffee at breakfast. There were dark rings round her eyes and she didn't bother with notices. She called out several people for uniform violations, snapped at the Ghost for gliding in a couple of minutes late, and sat nursing her coffee rather than patrolling the dining hall. It was pleasing to think Calding was finding Pankhurst life tiring just a few days into the term. She was going to be disappointed to find Meribel, Lo and I weren't going to take on any of the duties she'd outlined in her talk.

Meribel had secured us a table that was the next best thing to being empty. Other than three seats for us, it was completely taken by panicking fourth-formers, who had a science test and were caught up in shooting questions at each other and so weren't interested in anything we had to say.

"Tell us something juicy from your little outing, then," said Lo, after Meribel had hurriedly filled her in on me absconding for a couple of hours with Monro, but only because I couldn't sleep and had stepped out on to the fire escape. There'd been nothing prearranged, Meribel assured her, as if it might have been a betrayal if I had planned it without informing them.

The first thing I thought of was Monro's revelation about Veronica's artwork. "Er. . . I don't know."

"Come on!" said Meribel. "Is he really that boring?"

"You're a disappointment, Miss Jordan-Ferreira," said Lo, lifting her auburn hair with both hands, then holding it with one hand to place it all down one side of her neck. "Haven't you got *anything* decent to share with us?"

I opened my mouth a fraction.

Lo moved her upper body in time to imaginary music and pointed at me. "You have! I can tell!"

Looking round the dining hall, I checked to see if Veronica was there. Davison sixth-formers were allowed to come to Pankhurst for breakfast if they wanted something other than toast or cereal, which they could make in their little kitchen area, but they rarely bothered. "There was something," I said quietly, "But you have to keep it to yourselves. Promise?"

"Oooh, promise," said Meribel.

Lo said, "Yeah, yeah, I promise on my brother's life."

113

"Veronica's collage is interactive," I said quietly. "It's part of the project. According to Monro, *she* pinned up the prescription and the article. She wants people to join in."

They looked puzzled as my words sank in.

"Veronica wants everyone to post other people's secrets on her collage?" said Meribel. "Is she for real?"

"She did that to Zeta for an art project?" says Lo in a high voice. There's redness on her cheeks.

"Shhh," I said. "Monro says she thought the prescription was harmless, and she found it in the pigeonholes."

Lo made a snorting sound. "It was *private*. And to pick on Zeta. . ."

"Veronica's misjudged it," I agreed, but although that's what I thought, I wasn't going to be the one to spoil her project by revealing her secret to other students. At least not yet. I wondered if the housemistress in Davison knew about it. "Listen, let's keep it on the down-low for now." I looked at the other two, waiting until they nodded.

"She's encouraging us to snitch on each other though, isn't she?" said Meribel.

"Sort of, I suppose." I submerged three Cheerios under the milk in my cereal bowl with the round side of my spoon. Only one of them rose to the surface to the side of it. I'd have to hope the reveals didn't get out of control. It would be OK if the project became fun, not nasty.

"Why's she doing it?" asked Lo. "Did Monro say?"

I shook my head.

"Let's pin something up," I said. "We'll make it something amusing. Not embarrassing."

"So sadly that rules out a photo of you snogging Bernard then," said Meribel.

"Also, it doesn't exist," I said. "Thank God."

"Let's find something about Veronica," said Lo. "Give her a taste of her own medicine."

"No," said Meribel. "Clemmie. In the first form, she had a secret crush on those brothers with the pink wigs who thought they could rap. D'you remember, Lo? She swore she hated them but she was listening to them in the junior common room that time when she hadn't pushed her earphones into the socket of her phone properly."

I smiled at how embarrassed Clemmie must have been. "Were they the ones who had that big hit and went spectacularly bankrupt because they bought some restaurants and had no idea how to run them?"

Lo said, "Yeah. And we'd heard Clemmie tell everyone that Zeta was such a loser for listening to their stuff. Zeta had never even heard of them."

"I'm going to Photoshop a photo of her standing next to them," said Meribel.

"Nice idea," I said.

Since Calding didn't seem to be in a fighting mood that day, I took the opportunity to drag the others into the office with me to tell her we didn't want to take on any extra duties. I was ready with excuses about the volume of work in the fifth form but she didn't ask for reasons. She did her thing of pulling her thumb and forefinger over the corners of her mouth before removing them to say, "I'm not surprised, to be honest. You Pankhurst girls have so much potential, but you can be so selfish. Such enormous egos and lack of social responsibility."

We were taken aback by that.

In art, I began the preparation of paper clay. I added a couple of rolls of toilet paper in a bucket of water and let it soak, swishing it a bit while it disintegrated. When it had completely pulped I would add it to white clay, but in the meantime I made a structure from soft wire. It was the loose outline of a pair of hands that ended at the wrist, which I would cover with the paper clay. I worked from a photo of an elderly person's hands. I imagined them as Elsie Gran's. I'd ask her to get Maria next door to take a photo of them and send it to me.

"Did you know your mouth hangs open when you concentrate?"

I knew it was Bernard before I turned my head.

"Yes, I've been told that before," I said.

"It makes you look like you're about six." He picked up my pliers, and opened and closed them. "These look sharp."

"Give them here," I said, and held out my hand. "Got to clip off the end of this wire."

"You were probably pretty cute at six," he said.

I clipped the wire with more force than I needed to. I remembered being six. It was the first time I felt ugly.

"I was talking to Tessa Malone about your party," said Bernard. "She told me she'd been invited. I'm not going round blabbing, in case that's what you were thinking. Anyway, she thought fireworks over the cliff at midnight would be cool. What d'you think? She'll get her mum to have some delivered if you like."

Fireworks would be perfect. "D'you know how to set them off?" I asked. "Without killing anyone?"

"Of course. I help my uncle with his firework display every year. Leave it with me. I'll get you a price first then sort it."

Mr Hayes was nearly at my desk, on his rounds to see what we were all working on.

"Better go and do something arty, I suppose," Bernard muttered.

"Thanks for the fireworks," I said.

"No problem. Here for your every party need," he said and saluted. "I want you to have the party you deserve."

CHAPTER 14

It took Meribel a couple of days to get her Photoshopped picture right. She'd done an intricate job of making it look as if Clemmie had her arm round one of the rappers. She'd given her a pink jumper to match the boys' hair and a cheerleading pom-pom. In the meantime other things had appeared on Veronica's collage, among them a pale blue lacy bra, an article about nose-picking, a leaflet from a clinic for sexually transmitted diseases, and a stern written comment from a teacher ripped off the bottom of someone's history essay, all fastened with drawing pins purloined from other noticeboards around the school. Lo reckoned Veronica was responsible for them all. It was hard to tell.

Monro found his driving licence up there and swore loudly. At least he had one, I supposed.

"Yeah, you look pretty ropey in that photo, mate," said Bernard, and Monro had ignored him.

I hadn't had a chance to be with Monro on my own again since Thornley harbour. He'd been in Davison common room at the same time as me, but had been preoccupied. One time he'd been buried in a book, which was unusual because this was the common room, and not a study area. He had glanced up and smiled briefly, before folding over a corner of a page, then flipping to the back, as if an index was the most riveting reading material ever. When he left the common room, he pushed it under the armchair he was sitting on. Curious, I fished it out and saw it was an old paperback from the library upstairs, last taken out seven years ago: *Hidden Treasures: 100 Places to Explore in the British Isles.* The folded-over page was of a map of Great Britain. As I pushed it back under the chair, I wondered if he'd only been reading it so he could listen in to other people's conversations, or to avoid talking to me.

Meribel snuck out of school to go to Davison at lunchtime to position her printout, and came back to where we were sitting in the rose garden. She said she'd nearly been run over by Calding driving too quickly away from Pankhurst, not that Calding had noticed.

"Where d'you think she was going?" asked Lo.

"Who knows? That woman is so uptight I don't know how she doesn't explode," said Meribel. "Her body

119

language says she's not enjoying being housemistress. Trust me, over the summer, I watched loads on YouTube about body language. I'm going to take bets on when she resigns. She won't make it to the end of the term."

"Hope not," I muttered.

Lo said, "You don't think Calding is working undercover, do you?"

"What sort of undercover?" I asked.

"Dunno," said Lo. "Perhaps she's a school inspector or journalist. Or police."

"You might be on to something, Lo," said Meribel. "I've heard she's a rubbish science teacher."

"And she's been trying to recruit fifth-formers to run the science club she's supposed to be in charge of," said Lo. "Like she can't be bothered."

"We should definitely keep an eye on her," I said. Lo's theory made Calding a whole lot more interesting.

My phone vibrated with an email notification. I only ever received emails from school, and I was supposed to pick them up in the evening when I had permission to be on my phone. They were usually about class assignments or club information, but not this time.

"Oh, fabulous," I said sarcastically. "I have to give a visitor a tour of the school on Saturday morning. Saturday? I don't even get to miss lessons." I swiped it open and read out loud, *"Dear Kate, as House Prefect of Pankhurst, you are requested to* blah blah blah. . . Oh, wait, this isn't so bad."

"Sounds like a drag to me," said Meribel.

I shook my head. "Listen: *You and House Prefect of the Lower School at Churchill will meet Mr Lee in reception.*"

"House Prefect of the Lower School at Churchill – that's Hugo!" said Lo.

I nodded. "Correct. Not so bad. In fact, bring it on."

We wanted to be there when Clemmie saw herself Photoshopped. We followed her and Paige over to Davison, bunching closer to them as they walked through the door. There were already a few people there, mostly sitting at tables. Veronica was squishing a teabag against a mug in the kitchen. Hugo was by her artwork, looking at the picture.

"What's that, Hugo?" called Paige. Seeing if there was anything new on the collage had become something most of us did on walking into the common room.

"Something silly," said Hugo. He sounded dismissive, but I saw him look at Clemmie nervously as she and Paige came closer.

Clemmie stared at the photo and her face reddened.

"That's so funny," said Paige. "Look at you, Clem. I remember that group. What was their name again? They were your guilty pleasure."

Someone called out, "RapBros."

"What's all that about?" asked Flo.

"What's any of it about?" called Bernard. He was throwing crisps at another boy in our year. "I'd like to know about the bra, though."

Clemmie yanked the printout off the collage, so the

121

drawing pin that was attaching it pinged off on to the floor.

"Who put this up?" she demanded. She spun round. "Who was it?"

"What's the matter, Clem?" said Paige in a soothing voice. "Someone's just done it for a laugh."

Clemmie ripped it up, chucked it in the bin and walked out, nearly colliding with Monro as he came in.

"That was extreme," murmured Lo.

Meribel nodded slowly. "Talk about oversensitive."

The following day I skipped lunch and went to the art room instead. Under the watchful eyes of my dragons in the cabinet, I mixed my paper pulp into prepared clay. In the firing process the paper fibres would burn away, leaving lighter clay. I kneaded the mixture, and thought about Hugo. We had a connection. Doing the tour together on Saturday was an opportunity to get to know him better.

The art room was empty apart from a technician who had his earbuds in and was singing along to the *Hamilton* soundtrack. When I heard the door squeak open, I thought it was Meribel or Lo, coming to persuade me to sit outside with them in the September sunshine.

"I want to get this done," I said.

"Kate?"

I swung round to see Calding. What was she doing here? The science department was in a completely separate part of the building.

"Is my granny OK?" I asked, saliva drying up as I

suddenly thought of Elsie Gran. She'd messaged me in the morning, but anything could happen in the space of a few hours.

Ms Calding nodded. She pulled a stool from under the desk parallel to mine. I needed to scrape the clay from my hands and wash them, but the desire to know what she had to say was greater.

"It's about a letter," said Calding. I hated her over-serious manner at the best of times, but she was taking it too far now with the slowed-down speech and pauses. "It was sent to your grandmother's house from the father of a former student."

My hands found their way back to clay, and I started kneading. So Sasha's dad had found my address too.

"And your grandmother sent it on to us. It says you had something to do with his daughter's expulsion last term. Sasha Mires."

I wished Elsie Gran had warned me, but she probably hadn't thought it was worth bothering me with.

Calding reached into the pocket of her jacket. I stopped kneading and watched her pull out a folded piece of paper. I could see Elsie Gran's writing, made by a black ballpoint pen pressing too hard. Calding handed it to me and I held it at the very edges, so as not to get clay on it.

To whom it may concern,

My granddaughter, Kate Jordan-Ferreira, would certainly not be involved in anything like this. The school should be aware of this defamatory letter.

Elsie Jordan

She'd spoilt the sternness by adding a peace symbol. I turned the page over and saw the typed letter from Mr Mires. I skim-read it, taking in the words, *falsely accused of stealing an exam paper, slur on her character, devastating effect, your granddaughter needs to speak up if she knows something, school negligent, formal apology...* I clamped the inside of my cheek with my teeth, and handed the letter back.

"I'm trying to get to the bottom of this," said Calding.

The clay was drying on my hands, making them look ghostly. Trying to keep myself occupied, I wrapped the big lump on the round wooden board in front of me in a section of plastic sheeting so it didn't lose any more moisture.

"Tell me what you know," said Calding.

"Did you read my statement?" I asked. "It's all there." It felt as if my hair was sticking to the back of my neck with sweat.

Calding encouraged me to repeat how Clemmie had come to my room to do some of our geography project together, and that she'd left before Lo was back from dance club. She asked if we'd chosen to be partners for the geography project.

I looked at her bony face, and frowned. "No," I said.

124

"We didn't want to be partners, but we had to get it done."
It was the most truthful thing I'd said. We hadn't got a
good mark for that project on urbanization. We'd worked
on our parts separately on our laptops and I'd pieced it
together.

Did Sasha's parents know I'd provided an alibi for Clemmie?
"Has Sasha's dad been sending these letters to everyone?"
I asked.

Calding shook her head. "I don't know. Your
grandmother is the only person who's told us they received
one." She settled back on her stool. "I've spoken to Mr
Mires. He says his daughter never stole anything, and had
never seen that exam paper before."

"I heard Sasha's login was used on the teacher's laptop,"
I said. I'm not sure why I did because I knew what Calding
would come back with.

"That doesn't mean it was Sasha who logged in, does it?
Someone might have known her password."

"I guess it's possible," I said.

"Whoever logged into the laptop in Miss Wibberton's
office was a boarder at Pankhurst," said Calding. "The
CCTV camera at the front door didn't show anyone
coming into the building who shouldn't have been
there."

I thought of telling her it was easy to bypass the CCTV
at the back of Pankhurst, but for obvious reasons that
wasn't a sensible move.

She continued, "If you can think of anything you

125

might have forgotten to tell me, anything at all, please let me know."

I nodded. The conversation was over. I'd survived it.

"OK," said Calding. "Please tell your grandmother we've spoken about this." She stood up and hitched her trousers up by the waistband. I caught a glimpse of her pale flat stomach underneath the stripy shirt and navy jacket, taut like the rest of her.

I couldn't concentrate on the sculpture after she'd left. I picked up the board, placed it in the corner of the cupboard and went to find the others, who were stretched out on the empty cricket pitch, their heads resting on rolled-up blazers.

"I'm trying to persuade Lo to become an influencer," said Meribel. "She'd do a far better job than our dear friend Clemmie."

"The things I want to influence can't be monetized," said Lo. "Equality, tolerance..."

"Oh, purlease." Meribel lifted her arms up and blocked out the sun with her crossed-over hands. "I was sent a bikini for free last week by a company I modelled for. Retail value: £195. They want me to post a photo of myself wearing it."

"Are you going to do it?" I asked.

Meribel shook her head and shifted on to her elbow. "Not without the right backdrop. I'm not taking a photo of myself in my bedroom here. You can have it if you like, Lo. It's floral, oranges and pinks."

I settled down beside Lo, head straight on to the soft grass because my blazer was in my locker so I didn't destroy it in the art room, and said, "You'd look good in it."

"I literally never wear florals," said Lo, flicking the side of my face gently. "Why are you being so nice?"

I breathed in the sweet scent of the grass, "Because... What can I say, Freckle-Face? I want you to like me," I said.

Lo squeezed my hand. "So needy, Kate Jordan-Ferreira."

CHAPTER 15

School wanted as many students as possible to attend a talk by a motivational speaker in the assembly hall on Friday evening after dinner, but hardly anyone from Pankhurst apart from Lo and Zeta could be bothered to trudge back up to school and hear how some climber had survived a night in an ice crevice. Meribel said she'd seen a film that sounded very similar so there was no point, and I knew I couldn't sit and listen to someone who'd done heroic things. Not tonight when I couldn't stop thinking about the letter Sasha's dad had sent to Elsie Gran, and Elsie Gran's total conviction that I was innocent.

Bel and I watched a film in her room, and came downstairs when we knew cookery club would be offering

tasters of what they'd made. This week it was bite-si.
quiches, which tasted like bland scrambled egg in pastry.
Back upstairs, we were joined by Lo, and settled down
together to watch our favourite *Vampire Diaries* episode,
shushing Lo from time to time as she remembered
gruesome details from the climber's speech.

"You're quiet, Kate," said Meribel, when it was over
and we'd hopped on to YouTube.

"Thinking about your date with Hugo?" suggested Lo.

I rolled my eyes. "Give me a break. I'm tired, that's all."

Out of nowhere came a scream which reverberated
through the floor. We looked at each other, flung the
duvet back and ran to the stairs as the screams continued,
on and on. I reached the stairs first and scrambled down
faster than I ever had, looking to see what was happening
as soon as the second floor landing came into view.
Girls were running from every direction and I could see
something was going on either inside or outside Clemmie's
bedroom.

I pushed my way through, girls parting for me. I was
House Prefect, and I was aware of Meribel and Lo, my
deputies, right behind me.

Paige was lying on the floor, inside Clemmie's room,
moving a slow, shaky hand to her head. Clemmie was
kneeling next to her. She'd stopped screaming now but
was crying hysterically.

"What happened? Are you OK?" I asked Paige,
crouching beside her, but she didn't answer. "Has someone

gone to get Calding?" I checked with the girls behind me. They nodded.

"She was electrocuted," said Zeta in a wobbly voice. She stood by door. "I thought she was dead."

"What the hell. . .?" muttered Meribel.

I beckoned Zeta in. "Did you see it?" I asked her.

She nodded and gulped away a sob. "I was walking past."

"Calding's here," someone said.

"Out of the way, girls," Calding called, her voice authoritative. "Move! Move! Don't block the door. An ambulance is on its way."

Everyone moved back, including me, and Calding rushed over to Paige. "It's going to be OK."

"My head hurts," said Paige in a slurry voice. "Is it bleeding?"

Calding took a look. "No, but you've been knocked out. Stay still." She turned to Clemmie. "Stop that dreadful noise and tell me what happened."

Clemmie breathed in and out noisily a few times, and then said, "We'd been at Davison. We were going into my room. Paige turned on the light. Next thing she was flung across the room. She hit her head. She could have died. It was this one." She indicated the one just inside her door.

"Don't touch it!" boomed Squirrel's voice. I hadn't noticed her come upstairs. She was wearing a cardigan over her kitchen uniform and smelled of the spaghetti bolognaise we'd had at dinner. She went into Clemmie's room. "Metal light switch. Not good."

Calding stood up. "Girls, you're not to touch any electrics." She said to Squirrel, "Turn off the electricity immediately. Call the emergency electrician number in my office. I'm going to stay with Paige. The rest of you, please get ready for bed. There's just enough natural light to see what you're doing." She made a shooing movement with her hands.

"The girls need strong, sweet tea," said Squirrel. "Especially you and you." She pointed to Clemmie and Zeta. "Come downstairs. We'll make tea in Davison if we need to."

All of us went downstairs into the dining hall, thrilled that Squirrel had overruled Calding and Calding had said nothing, buzzing with what had happened. There was no way we could have just gone to bed.

Clemmie had to be helped downstairs by a couple of her group. "It could have been me," she said. "It was my room. Oh my God. I could have hit my head worse than Paige. Or I could have a heart condition that I don't know about and died."

The ambulance and the electrician came at the same time, as Squirrel and Davison staff ferried big teapots back and forth. We dunked Digestive biscuits into our mugs of tea and traded stories of disasters. We saw the paramedics lead Paige downstairs. Calding followed and went in the ambulance with her to hospital. If it had been me, I'd have asked for Squirrel instead.

Squirrel asked me to take up a mug of tea for the electrician. "Milk and one sugar, as he requested," she said.

As I got closer to Clemmie's room, walking slowly so I didn't spill the tea, I heard him on the phone, explaining he would be late to something because he was on an emergency call-out.

"Loose wire against the metal box," he said. "A kid got hurt. . ." He paused to let the other person speak. "Yeah, metal switch. Old building." Another pause. "Yeah, that's also a possibility." Pause. "Too extreme? Yeah, you're right, mate. Won't mention that. New housemistress is panicked enough as it is."

I waited outside, watching the steam from the tea rise, hoping there was more to hear. What was too extreme? Who was the electrician to decide what to mention and what to keep quiet about? He finished the call with a "Catch you later" rolled into one word, and I heard him whistle cheerily.

"Here you go," I said as I walked in. He'd replaced the metal light switch to a plastic one and was putting his tools away.

"Oooh, lovely, thanks," said the electrician, taking the mug and gulping a mouthful.

I didn't think there was any harm asking. "Could someone have done something to the old switch deliberately?" I asked.

The man's cheeriness faded. "Why d'you ask?" Was he worried that I'd overheard his conversation? "Do you know anything?"

I shook my head. "Just wondering."

"Nah, I doubt it." He found his grin again. "Thanks again for my tea."

Paige came back in a taxi with Calding before breakfast the following morning, showing everyone the tiny burn mark on her finger, and clutching her box of painkillers, happy to have everyone fussing round her, coming downstairs to see her in their dressing gowns. Calding looked shattered, and went straight to bed after a chat with the Ghost.

I ate breakfast in a hurry, self-conscious in my school uniform on a Saturday, but ready to give Mr Lee his tour of Mount Norton. I hoped Hugo was going to call in at Pankhurst so we could walk together but he didn't, and in the end I had to jog to reach the reception for the time I'd been given on the email. Hugo was perched on the edge of a desk in the side office with two female members of the reception staff, and they were laughing at some story he was telling them about a restaurant.

"This is such a drag, isn't it?" he said when he saw me.

"Totally," I said, and examined his face. Everything about it was naturally symmetrical. My father would be hard-pressed to suggest any improvements to it.

I signed in and listened as Hugo finished up the story, which ended up with a waiter being sacked, and then the two of us left the office to sit and wait for Mr Lee in reception, sitting on the dark wooden bench with the red-velvet cushioned seat. I took a mental selfie of us, moving towards Hugo a fraction as I imagined the photo. We made a good couple.

Hugo described the route we should take round the school. It wasn't the most logical one, but it would do. One of the receptionists went out to greet Mr Lee as a long, black car drew up outside. She brought him in and introduced us. He bowed to each of us, and explained he'd heard such wonderful things about Mount Norton and wanted to see it for himself before he came with his son. Hugo led the way. He also led the talking, and left no gaps for me. When I chipped in, he frowned. When I tried another time, he said, "Kate, can you wait until I've finished what I was going to say?"

As we waited in the science corridor for Mr Lee to read a display, I said in a low voice, "Why aren't you letting me say anything?"

Hugo looked surprised. "I am letting you, but I don't like it when you interrupt. It's rude."

I felt a tight bubble of anger expand in my head. "Then we should take turns."

He pulled an I'm-embarrassed-to-have-to-tell-you-this face. "I know, I know, but can't you tell I've got a better rapport with Mr Lee than you have?"

"No," I said. "He listens to me when I get a word in."

"Of course, but—"

"You're saying there's no point me being here, then?"

Hugo glanced at Mr Lee, who was still reading, then

said, "Kate, you add the wow factor. You're essential."

Heat flared on my face. "What?"

"You're a great advert for the school."

He wasn't going to say it outright, that if I looked different I wouldn't have been chosen, not now he'd seen the look in my eyes.

Mr Lee walked up to us and said he was ready to move on. We went into the art wing and into my art room. I opened my mouth to describe the different art opportunities at the school, but Hugo beat me by a split second. He was very clever and extremely sporty but he didn't take art as a subject.

"I'm better qualified on this," I said. "I'll start off."

Hugo gave a fake little laugh, and made a comedy apologetic face at Mr Lee.

I paused, like a teacher might for silence, and he shot me a look. It meant, *don't you dare cause a scene.*

I'd got Hugo wrong. I hadn't really misinterpreted the last twenty minutes, had I? It made me dizzy, knowing something but not fully able to believe it.

Mr Lee was smiling. He thought this was a well-rehearsed double act.

I took a deep breath as I looked at my dragons in the cabinet, and then I spoke about the art room.

CHAPTER 16

I didn't come straight back to Pankhurst. I went on to the cliff path and walked up to the beach house, stopping by a gap in the foliage where at sunset people liked to take selfies with the sea in the background. I needed to be on my own, away from Hugo, and not yet back at Pankhurst explaining to Lo and Meribel how disappointed I was, and how strangely ashamed I felt that I'd built him up so much. The steady in and out of the waves was calming.

Meribel was in Ryemouth when I returned, but Lo listened to me, and said she understood how people could turn out not to be who you thought they were even when you'd known them for years. I knew she was thinking about Sasha, and that made me feel worse, so I said I needed to blast away my thoughts by dancing to a Monsta X track.

"Dancing is usually the answer," replied Lo, as she cleared space on her bedroom floor and we assumed positions for the start of "Alligator".

The talk in Davison over the next few days was mainly about Paige's electric shock, and whether her parents would sue the school. Paige said they were taking legal advice. Clemmie said her parents were also speaking to their lawyer because it was her light switch.

"I need financial compensation too," she muttered.

"Quite right," said Hugo.

Monro had looked up from his tatty *Hidden Treasures* book and said it wasn't a proper short circuit so it wouldn't have killed Clemmie, and Clemmie had stood up from the armchair she'd been curled up in, cheeks blazing, and said she couldn't believe he could say that when there were all sorts of things she might have knocked her head on, or medical issues she wasn't aware of.

Monro had shrugged and gone back to his book, and Hugo said smoothly, "Don't let him wind you up, Clem."

We'd only spoken once since the school tour. Hugo had found me in the main school dining hall the Monday after and said he was sorry if I felt he'd taken over the tour. He could see why I might have thought that, but he'd heard from Miss Sneller that Mr Lee had been very taken with the school, so it had worked out in the end.

"So we're cool?" he'd finished up with. He'd given me his full-attention, perfect smile.

"I'll think about it," I said and he'd laughed that same ridiculous fake laugh.

A receipt for a dress appeared on Veronica's artwork. Other receipts joined it as the news drip-dripped out about my beach-house party, alongside more embarrassing items such as a delivery note for some stick-on underarm sweat patches and a Polaroid of some firm-control shaping knickers.

The dress code didn't need to be specified; it was always smart for boarding-house parties. I'd bought a dress in Italy over the summer, exclusive to a small label, which Meribel had given me the green-light on via video link. She herself was vacillating between four outfits she'd express-imported from the States. Lo was adapting an old dress of her mother's. She'd slashed the neck and hemline in the textiles studio.

I watched her sew beads on top of the ribbon she was going to cover the neck seams with. She and I were in her bedroom listening to a band her friends back home had told her about, and I was flicking through shoe websites on my phone. Meribel was FaceTiming her boyfriend in her room next door, and we could hear her giggling through the wall.

"I've got something to confess," said Lo. She rolled a bright blue bead between her thumb and forefinger. She kept her eyes on the bead, and said, "I texted Sasha an invitation to your party." In the pause that followed she raised her eyes. "I know I should have asked you, but I want to see her, and the party's a good excuse. I don't care what she's done any more. I know she was clever enough to do well in that exam without cheating."

"But she lied to your face."

"The more I think about it, the more I think she must have had a good reason that she couldn't tell me about."

"Has she replied?" I asked. I sounded too urgent, but I needed to stop the thudding of my heart. I hadn't told her about the letters Sasha's dad had sent to Elsie Gran and Clemmie's parents. I didn't want Lo to know Sasha's parents were convinced she hadn't stolen the exam paper.

"Not yet," said Lo. "I said I was sorry about not being in contact. I told her she could stay over at the beach house if she wanted, or we'd smuggle her up the fire escape here." She looked at me, willing me to be OK about it.

"Sure," I said. My heart still thumped. Sasha wouldn't come. Why would she want to return here? Unless . . . she had something she wanted to say? I had to delve into Lo's plastic container of beads to find a silver one, the next colour she needed in her bead sequence, because I couldn't bear to see her hopeful smile.

"I hope she turns up," she said. "I really don't care what anyone else thinks." She pushed the needle through the tiny hole of the bead and stitched it on. "People have done worse things at this school, they just haven't been caught."

"I know," I said. I held out a silver bead, tiny like a crumb in my outstretched palm.

The preparations for the party, and the stress, mounted. I fell asleep exhausted each night but woke early, stepping out on to the fire escape to see if Monro was there, but he didn't seem to be waking early any more. I'd have liked to have seen him.

Veronica told me Monro was happy to take a Churchill sixth-former who was already eighteen in his car to pick up alcohol for the party. She gave me Monro's number and told me to sort it out with him directly.

I called him one night to talk through the logistics of payment, quantities and delivery. "It's a big thing, organizing a boarding-house party," he said after I told him I was worried I might have forgotten something. "Sounds to me as if you've got everything covered though."

"I want people to think it was as good as Veronica's rooftop one," I said.

"Yeah," said Monro. "Didn't you and Bernard end up together that time?"

I closed my eyes in embarrassment, even though he wasn't in the same room as me. "Er . . . sort of," I said faintly.

"I ended up needing an X-ray on my ankle," said Monro. "Mixed feelings about the party, really."

After Bernard and I had kissed, we'd danced together

140

for a bit, Meribel and Lo giving me amused glances and thumbs-up, and Bernard mouthing lyrics incorrectly. After a while, he wanted to walk down the beach where it was quiet and dark, but I shook my head and asked if he'd fetch me a drink.

I was on my own on the edge of the dance area when Clemmie approached me. Meribel and Lo were concentrating on a complicated dance routine, and weren't looking my way. What Clemmie had to say didn't take long.

"I need you to do something for me." I saw her eyes hard and shining in the half-light, checking around us to see if we could be overhead. "If anyone happens to ask, we were doing our geography project on Friday after dinner, until just before Lo came back from whatever she does on a Friday evening."

"I have no clue what you're talking about," I said. "We still need to work on that project."

"We're doing it separately," said Clemmie quickly. "But you'll say I was with you on Friday after dinner." I didn't understand how she was so certain I'd agree until she said, "I know about you, Kate. I have a photo of you."

The surprise made my mouth open. I fought for words. "How?" I asked.

"Hopefully no one will ask you about Friday, but if they do, you know what to say. Right?" Clemmie had been so smoothly confident.

Monro's voice cut into the replaying of the scene.

"Kate? Are you still there?"

"Yes, sorry. I was distracted by a wasp in my room." It was the first excuse I could think of.

"Oh. I'd better let you go," said Monro.

"Yes, OK. Bye then," I said. I stared at my screen for a few moments after the call ended. I wished I'd concentrated more on what he'd been saying to me. That way, he might not have wanted to hang up so soon.

He texted early the next morning to see if I was awake and wanted to walk to the beach.

I am and yes, I texted back.

He met me outside Pankhurst's back gate. It was misty and colder than it had been so far this term, and I was pleased to see he had the red thermos with him. I had half a packet of Oreos.

We walked on the coastal path to the beach house, and I was startled to see a man in a pink polo shirt looking out of one of the top-floor windows. He stared at us, and I was the one who looked away first.

"He's in my house," I said indignantly, and Monro laughed.

We carried on until the steps, and Monro told me how he'd almost fallen down them one winter when it was icy, and he'd experienced the life-flashing-before-your-eyes phenomenon. "All these memories came tumbling out. I really thought I was a goner."

"Good memories, though?" I asked.

He nodded. "Mostly, but I need to stack up more of them. I want a longer showreel next time." He put down his thermos, took hold of the rails either side of the steps, and lifted his legs off the ground, swinging them back and forth as if he were doing a gym exercise. If he let go, he'd definitely fall and would probably never get up again.

I picked up the thermos and ran a third of the way down the steps, sat down and unscrewed the lid. By the time I'd poured out some tea and taken a sip, he was beside me. "Will this be a good memory?" I asked, waving my arm around to take in the scene, the mist making the beach colours more muted than usual, and a dog leaping around by the water's edge, his owner out of sight but whistling furiously. "Having me in it too, obviously?" I raised my eyes.

"Of course," he said. "Classic showreel material."

We were definitely flirting.

We took it in turns to dunk the Oreos in the tea. It wasn't warm enough to sit for long, so after we'd finished the biscuits, we had a race to the bottom of the steps. I won easily, and Monro said it was because he was carrying the thermos, which was the most pathetic excuse I'd ever heard.

"I'm in such a good mood, I feel like singing," I announced. I demanded a song request from him, pushing him for more until he came up with one I knew all the words to. It was liberating to sing as loudly as I wanted into the wind, for my audience of one, who grinned as if I was mad, but also as if he liked it. We picked our way along the beach where the stones nestled in the damp sand, but the waves didn't reach our trainers.

The beach café was closed, but I could see a light on at the back and Kipper's bicycle chained up down the side.

I stopped singing and said, "Kipper gives me the shivers."

"Stay away from him," said Monro.

I laughed at his earnest face. "Don't worry, M. I like that you care, though!" I'd called him M, like I occasionally heard Veronica do. It gave me a strange feeling, as if I'd stepped on something I hadn't noticed and might have crushed.

We walked up the zigzag path and across the car park to check nobody had broken into Monro's car.

"You wouldn't believe how much I love this car," said Monro, touching the bonnet.

"You're literally stroking it," I said. "I can't watch." I walked off towards Pankhurst and he caught up, putting his arm round me for a brief, surprising second and squeezing me, before removing it as we walked the last couple of hundred metres home.

Clemmie paid me a visit the following evening on the third floor.

"I thought I'd drop by," she said as she slipped into my room, arriving so quietly at my door she made me jump.

I had been struggling with an essay about Shakespeare's use of language in *Macbeth* at my desk, and Meribel and Lo hadn't clocked her coming in. She was dressed in pink silky pyjamas, and her blonde hair was piled high on her head. Her face was gleaming, like a sweet little YouTuber who'd just filmed a skincare routine.

"I hope you haven't been talking about things you shouldn't have," she said now. "Calding pulled me out of a Spanish class today to speak to me about Sasha."

I bit the end of my ballpoint pen as she spoke. When she'd finished, I removed it to say, "She spoke to me too. Sasha's dad wrote my grandmother a letter."

"Oh," said Clemmie. Her face relaxed a little, and then tightened. "Because I have the perfect place to post my photo of you before your operations if you change your story."

She walked out and banged the door, and I dropped my head to my hands. If people saw a photo of me when I was little they would gawp and laugh, and it would never be over.

I'd become a new version of myself, and I was ashamed how much I liked it. I was Kate Jordan-Ferreira, effortlessly beautiful and therefore powerful at this school. I couldn't let anything change that. I picked up my phone and searched for the old number I still had in my contacts for Sasha, and texted: *Don't come to the Pankhurst party.*

CHAPTER 17

The day of the party I woke feeling uneasy, but I went downstairs with Lo for breakfast anyway, as a distraction, even though it was Saturday and I didn't need to.

There'd been no reply from Sasha. I hoped she'd changed her number, and hadn't received any of Lo's texts, or mine.

Sitting next to Lo, and hearing her say how excited she was at the possibility Sasha might turn up, made me incapable of eating my Saturday pancakes and maple syrup.

Most students seemed to know about the party even though only a fraction of them had been invited. Zeta wished me luck as we left the hall, and I almost told her she should drop by the beach house later to see it.

We waited until my godfather had forwarded us the code for the beach house's key safe before we woke Meribel. As we left Pankhurst with bulging shopping bags of decorations and party food, Calding stepped out of her office. She was with the Furball, who did random shifts when the Ghost wasn't around. The Furball often had a hacking cough, hence her name.

"Morning, girls." Calding eyed our bags. "What on earth have you got there?"

We'd thought of our answer in advance, but it made us sound like we were from the eighteenth century when Meribel said it. "Picnic stuff and art things. We're going up on the cliffs." We opened the bags to show her. The decorations were hidden at the bottom; the fireworks were being delivered by Bernard and Tessa, and the alcohol by Monro.

Calding glanced into them briefly. "I see. Have a good time."

"It's marvellous you girls are getting some fresh air," said the Furball.

Bernard and Tessa were waiting for us outside the beach house, next to a large cardboard box that was covered in *FRAGILE* stickers.

"The deluxe assortment," said Bernard with pride, as if he'd given birth to the fireworks.

"Just make sure you don't blow up the house," said Meribel.

Bernard tutted.

"This is so exciting," squealed Tessa.

I fumbled with the code on the key safe, my hand shaking a little. If I couldn't get to the keys, everything would be an utter disaster. The box sprung open, and a single key on a plain grey keyring sat there. It slid into the lock smoothly, and the door opened into an empty hall with white walls and light wood flooring. I let out my breath and hoped nobody had seen how tense I'd been.

The house had the thick, stuffy smell of a space that needed airing. Meribel went ahead of me, opening doors, exclaiming loudly at the size of the place and the stripped-back style, telling us it was going to look incredible in everyone's photos.

The large living room led to the kitchen in a big open-plan area. Everything was white, metal or smoothed driftwood. The Airbnb people had left a grey vase of white roses on the central island and two champagne flutes. In the American-style fridge was a small bottle of Moët. Nice touch.

We dumped our bags by the huge bi-fold doors. The garden looked even prettier from this viewpoint, with the dark-green cliff foliage behind it, and then the sea. The water was pale today, merging with the unsettled sky. Instead of opening the doors to the garden, we raced upstairs to the two double bedrooms and Bernard did a running jump on to one of them and told us to join him for a group hug. Tessa was the only one who did, and Bernard took a selfie of them together against the white pillows.

"Come on," I said. "Let's go downstairs. We've got to put up the decorations and the lights, and Monro will be here soon with the wine."

In the kitchen we lifted the shopping bags on to the central island to unpack. Tessa opened each cupboard and told us what it contained, which grew irritating very quickly. "We could put things on actual china plates! Make it really civilized?" she said.

I shook my head. This beautiful house felt like an enormous responsibility, and that feeling was only going to get worse as it filled up with people.

Lo said, "We've got paper plates, Tessa, and napkins. That's all we need."

I shot her a grateful look as the doorbell rang, and I rushed to answer it. I checked through the peephole first before flinging open the door to Monro and Veronica. Between them they had three wheel-along suitcases, carry-on luggage size.

"Two of these have alcohol in," said Monro.

"And the third one's mine," said Veronica. "Can I leave it upstairs for tonight? I want to get changed here after the Autumn Party. I'm giving a speech so I've got to wear something sensible to start off with."

"It looks as if you've come to stay," said Bernard.

"I've got a few outfits to choose from," said Veronica.

Meribel nodded. "Ah. Same. I have to wait and see what mood I'm in. Come on, I'll show you the bedrooms."

149

The rest of us led Monro into the front for the view.

"Ooh, nice," he said, pressing his face against the large glass doors.

"You're leaving smear marks," said Bernard. "Aren't you going to unpack the alcohol?"

"It's fine, Bernard," I said. I nearly added, *Leave him alone,* but I thought Monro didn't need me to stand up for him.

Monro acted as if he hadn't even heard. As Veronica came into the kitchen and joined him at the window, she said, "This place is fantastic, Kate." I caught the admiration in her voice, and I tucked it away to savour later.

The two of them eventually stepped away from the view and unloaded the bottles on to the central island. "We're happy to stay and help with whatever needs doing for a while," said Monro, as he zipped up the empty suitcases.

Bernard said, "We've got it covered."

"That would be great," I said. "I need help putting up the indoor lights."

"Sure," said Monro. His eyes met mine and my stomach flipped. He made my body do that just by looking at me. Bel and Lo would laugh if I told them how I was starting to feel about him.

"Veronica, d'you want to help me and Tessa put tea lights in those jars?" said Lo.

Meribel said she'd sort the sound system, and Bernard announced he was going to decide where to launch the fireworks from.

"Fireworks, huh?" said Monro.

"For midnight," I said. "I'm entrusting Bernard with them."

"You think it's wise to trust him?" said Monro. He was checking the joints of his hand, but looked up at me at the end of his sentence.

"Of course she does," said Bernard. He unlocked the end of the bifold doors and stepped out. He called back, "I think we'll cordon off that corner by the path."

I took the box of fairy lights from the work surface. "We'll start in the living room, on the far wall. I've got drawing pins and tape."

Monro picked up a stool from under the central island and carried it to the corner of the living room.

The stool wasn't very stable, so we took it in turns holding it for each other, until Veronica found a stepladder in a cupboard.

"Here you go," she said, as she opened it up and took the stool away.

"You're such a mum," said Monro, flicking her ponytail.

After we'd finished, and gathered everyone to admire the lights, Veronica said, "We have to go. We've got things to do, haven't we, Monro?" and I was absurdly jealous of the look that passed between them. It was secretive, and not at all maternal.

Later, when we'd finished placing the tea lights outside, I went upstairs to see what was in Veronica's suitcase.

Something felt off about it. She wasn't the sort of person to have multiple outfits for a party.

The suitcase was tucked under the bed. I had to lie on my stomach to reach it, and when I dragged it across the thick carpet, it was heavy. I didn't want to explain what I was doing to the others if they came upstairs so I fumbled quickly for the zip and tugged.

It was locked. I grimaced with embarrassment. Did Veronica guess I'd be nosy?

Bernard called me from the hall. "Come and see how I've decorated the garden for you."

I shoved the suitcase back. "I'm coming down," I shouted. At the top of the stairs, I said, "Shall I block off the bedrooms to stop them being trashed? They don't lock from the outside."

"Chill," said Bernard. "It's all going to be OK."

It would be. I came slowly downstairs, reminding myself that this party was going to be the best Mount Norton had ever seen.

CHAPTER 18

The Autumn Party took place, as all termly parties did, in the main school assembly hall. The multiple sets of French doors had been opened on to the old stone terrace. Waiters and waitresses circulated with trays of canapés, non-alcoholic punch for students under eighteen, and alcoholic drinks for anyone lucky enough to be issued a red wristband. A few outside adults, to do with the local council and various businesses that had links to the school, had been brought in for us to make polite conversation with. It was considered good training for life.

An hour or so into the evening Veronica made a speech about the school's glittering achievements in the previous term. She wore a gold jumpsuit, and her nervous energy made her more intense than usual. Hugo, representing the fifth-formers, revealed how much had been raised for charity in the same time period. He looked gorgeous in his suit but sounded smug. Had he always been so full of himself, or was it a recent thing?

"He's got worse," said Lo, reading my thoughts. "He used to be quite nice. What a waste of humanity."

I placed my arm round her shoulder and pulled her towards me with affection. "Couldn't agree more, Lo!" She looked incredible tonight with her copper hair piled on top of her head, wearing her cleverly altered dress with the beaded neckline. She and Sasha had made a stunning couple when they'd dressed up. I could almost feel Sasha's presence next to us, with her sharp haircut, endless legs and the mini-dress she'd worn to the rooftop party. I let go of Lo's shoulder.

Soon, the old people would be carted off for a formal dinner, the band would start up in the dining hall, and platters of less-fancy nibbles would be brought out. If you were a first- or second-former, it was grand and exciting. Otherwise it was so dead.

It was easy to disperse once the band started playing, as most of the teachers drifted off at that point, leaving core staff who tended to chat to each other by the entrance, to make sure once people left they didn't come back in. They also walked groups of students back to their boarding houses at set times, but fifth and sixth-formers were allowed to walk back on their own. The critical thing was signing back into your boarding house. And of course there were certain students with a talent for forgery who would sign anyone in for payment.

But Lo, Bel and I needed to leave far earlier; we would take the over-the-fence route. I had to be first to my own party, and I had another five minutes before I needed to leave. The problem was Calding. She was standing at the edge of the hall like part of the security team, watching everyone. She'd misjudged the dress code. While students dressed up, staff tended not to, and as a result she stood out in her seaweed-green shift dress. She'd done her make-up differently, more heavily, and combined with the try-hard dress, it made her seem much younger and more awkward.

The three of us stood by the open doors faking interest in a third-former's magic trick. I'd been standing still so long, I was beginning to feel cold.

"Yo!" said a voice in my ear. Monro. Veronica was nowhere to be seen. "I'm surprised you lot are still here."

I let out a sigh of frustration. "If Calding doesn't stop watching us, we're going to have to create a distraction."

"It's like she knows what we're up to," said Lo, pulling at a curl of escaped hair from her loose bun.

"That woman is a nightmare," said Meribel. "What is wrong with her?"

"Well, let's separate. Make it harder for her," said Monro. "I'll go outside with Kate and be her cover. We'll look as if we're going for a romantic wander. See you two later at the beach house."

"What?" I said.

He took my hand and led me outside where a school string quartet was playing show tunes. I didn't turn to see what anyone else thought. I went with him.

"Where's Veronica?" I asked.

"Phoning her mum," Monro said. He kept hold of my hand. The electric feeling of his skin against mine radiated up my arm and through my body.

We didn't speak as we walked towards the fence, past the little floodlit stone fountain, where it was customary for couples to have photos taken. There were lots of students milling around. It felt natural, walking hand in hand with Monro. We checked behind us before climbing over the fence in an area shielded by trees, and it was as easy as it had been the previous year.

It would have been weird to have held hands again on the other side of the fence. There wasn't a purpose to it any more. It would have meant something. The start of the coastal path was darker than I'd thought it would be, and we needed our phone torches to see. Monro tripped over a tree root, and as I went to grab him my right foot went sideways in my heels and I shrieked.

We laughed, and clung on to each other a moment.

"I wish I'd got to know you sooner, Kate," he said as we walked along at a slower pace, watching the ground more intently. "I always thought you were quite

156

intimidating before . . . and I guess I heard things from Clemmie's side."

"Intimidating, huh?" I said.

"And overwhelmingly beautiful," he added. "Maybe those things are connected. And maybe that's why Clemmie is bitter."

I shook my head as if to say let's not have this discussion. I had an urge to tell him the truth – about me, and about what Clemmie had done, and what I hadn't done – but he was still part of her home crowd, and his parents knew hers. I couldn't be sure of him.

As the path curved we saw the lights of the beach house. We hadn't left any candles burning, but we'd kept the fairy lights on, and the little lights embedded in the decking outside. It looked magical.

I gave a whoop. "Come on," I said and broke into as much of a run as I could in my heels. On unlocking the door I went to open the bifold doors on to the garden. The whoosh of the sea below the cliff seemed louder from here than it had when we were walking. I needed to light the tea lights in the jars we'd placed round the edge of the decking, but for a moment I wanted to lean against the door frame and breathe in the dark and light, and the feeling that I was Kate Lynette Jordan-Ferreira, for whom anything was possible, including throwing an illegal party in a romantic beach house with one of the best views in the world.

"It's nice, isn't it?" I said softly, looking round for Monro. I willed him to come closer, and he did. I opened my mouth the tiniest fraction, my lips separating, and I looked at him and I knew what my eyes were saying, and it seemed as if I'd stopped breathing as he lowered his lips very gently on mine as his answer.

I stood more upright, and leaned into him, circling his upper body with my hands, feeling the muscles of his back. His hands moved from my waist to my hips as our tongues met, and our deep kiss pulsed through my body

This. This was the feeling I hoped was possible. For a few seconds it was him and me and nothing else mattered or would ever matter until, like a radio being switched on, the shouts and laughter of people coming along the coastal path intruded, and I broke away.

"We're not ready," I said. I was fuelled by a rush of adrenaline as I put on the music and we lit the candles as fast as we could. We finished as the doorbell was rung repeatedly.

Everyone seemed to arrive together, a stream of people who excitedly admired the house and the view, and then fell upon the alcohol or opened up what they'd brought with them. Lo, Meribel and I hugged and shrieked together in the kitchen. This party was on!

Two rugby guys, Rob and Matty, said Bernard had asked them to be bouncers, but they'd need beer as payment.

"We'll cover outside. Give us a shout if anything kicks off inside," Rob said. "Anything at all." He rotated a shoulder, and the two of them went off with a stack of beer.

As I opened some packets of crisps to shove on to paper plates, the loud pop of the Moët bottle startled me. I saw Bernard swigging from it.

"Awesome party so far," he said. "And you're going to love the firework display."

"Yep, it's going to be good," I said. I pushed the empty packets in the bin, and slipped into the garden. The air smelled of candles, cigarette smoke, perfume and the sea. People stood in huddles, chattering and laughing. Lo and Meribel were waving sparklers with Tessa. I scanned for Monro but couldn't see him.

Someone came up behind me and said, "Not bad for a Pankhurst party."

I spun round, recognizing Hugo's voice.

"You're looking irresistible tonight," he drawled.

"*Bringing the wow factor* is just one of many skills," I said.

"Of course. Don't be prickly." He put his hand on my shoulder. "I won't let you go until you promise to dance with me later. Promise?"

I wriggled my shoulder and he took the hint and dropped his hand, a look of startled disgust on his face.

"Sorry, Hugo, I've got to find someone," I said and walked away.

I hadn't seen Monro since the first guests arrived. The whole of the downstairs was packed now, and I weaved in and out of the crowd, smiling and nodding like a party pro, like my mother would have done. Eventually I saw Monro talking to Veronica next to the shelving unit.

Their conversation looked intense. Veronica was still wearing the same jumpsuit she'd made her speech in, and I thought of her suitcase upstairs. She obviously couldn't be bothered to get changed.

Clemmie walked unsteadily past them, knocking into Veronica, which made Veronica spill some of her drink down her top. Clemmie was drunk already.

"Hey," said Veronica. "Careful." She muttered something to Monro.

"Oh, piss off," said Clemmie. "Stop giving me a hard time. I've had it with you and your family."

Veronica looked as if she'd been slapped. "How can you say that? My parents have done nothing but help, and look where it's got them."

"You'd better stop looking down your nose at me," spat Clemmie, stepping into Veronica's personal space.

I watched, appalled. Clemmie was making a fool of herself, which ordinarily I wouldn't mind, and I wished I knew what she was going on about, but she was ruining the ambience of my party.

"You'd better stop making things worse for yourself." Veronica gave Clemmie a push and she stumbled backwards.

"Whoa," said Monro. He caught Clemmie by the arm and stopped her falling. Clemmie shook him off, and Paige appeared, saying she'd been looking everywhere for her.

"Kipper's outside," Paige said. "I've told him you don't want to see him."

Clemmie slurred, "He's mad at me."

"Obsessed, you mean," said Paige.

"Tell him to go away," said Clemmie. She sounded tearful all of a sudden. "Please. Don't let him come in through the garden."

"Rob and Matty will chuck him out if he does," said Paige.

I couldn't imagine Kipper calling the police to tell them about the party, but if he was provoked he might. I went into the hall to see how Rob and Matty were handling the situation.

They were blocking his way in. As soon as Kipper saw me, he yelled, "Yo, Gorgeous! I need to speak with Clemmie. I know she's in there. Send her out here if you don't want me coming in."

"She doesn't want to see you," I said, furious with Clemmie. It seemed as if it was completely her fault he was here.

"Doesn't she?" Kipper acted surprised. "She was going to help me out."

Kipper shook free of Rob's arm on his, and said, "Tell her I'll catch up with her very soon."

He left, and Rob stuck his thick neck out, pleased with himself. "I think I just earned myself another drink there."

Going back into the party, everything was as it should be. People were having fun. I walked through the living room and kitchen, and stood against the metal doorframe looking into the garden, at everyone so animated, at the blurry golden glow of the lights, and the silent sticks of fireworks in the corner. Monro and Veronica had moved outside. They were sitting on the same stone step, their heads close together, talking. I should be next to him on that step, not her.

"You all right?" Lo was by my side. "You want a drink?"

I hadn't thought to have one. I'd been too busy. Lo reached for a clear plastic cup of Prosecco on the side which had already been poured. "Here."

I sipped, savouring the sharp, tight-bubbled sensation. I rarely drank Prosecco, and the first sip was always more bitter than I expected.

Lo's drink had a slice of lemon floating in it. I didn't remember anyone slicing lemons. The party felt as if it had its own momentum now, separate from my involvement. In the living room behind us, some people were dancing.

Bernard stepped from the garden into the kitchen. I elongated myself into the doorframe so he didn't touch me on his way past.

"I really thought Sasha might turn up here tonight," said Lo when Bernard had gone. "Stupid me. She was never going to come, was she?" She gazed at me through watery eyes.

I filled my lungs with traitorous breath and said, "I'm so sorry."

"It's OK," said Lo. "I need to move on. It's just . . . I feel as if I let her down."

"Please don't say that," I said, my words tumbling out in a gush of self-loathing. I was such a coward. I had to tell Lo about Sasha. But this wasn't the right moment; I'd tell her after the party, when I could explain it properly.

"This place," said Meribel, swooping past with a twelve-pack of crisps. "No one's going to top it, Kate."

I saw a movement on the path, and stepped into the garden with Lo to see. It was Kipper, smoking. He was half looking out to sea, half keeping an eye on what was happening in the garden.

"Is that Kipper again?" said Meribel. "He needs to stop hanging around a teenage party like a sleazeball." She walked a bit further to the very end of the garden and before I could stop her shouted, "Get lost, Kipper!" and rounded it off with a lot of swearing.

Everyone around us looked up as Kipper held up his hands and said, "Hey, I'm relaxing with a cigarette and minding my own business, if that's OK with you?"

"In the dark? While perving on us?" She looked around for support. "Anyone want to get Rob and Matty?"

Kipper ground his cigarette butt into the ground and said, "I'm going."

Meribel gave me a triumphant look, and a couple of seconds later there was the sound of someone puking into the bushes. It was Clemmie.

"That's going to be gross," said Lo. "It's gone in between those white pebbles."

"Hope it rains before the next renters come," I murmured.

We watched Paige ask a couple of people to move off a bench because Clemmie wanted to lie down, and when I looked away I saw Veronica coming towards me, and Monro was following her. Finally, they'd decided to be sociable.

"Kate," said Veronica. I couldn't work out the tone in her voice. She seemed nervous. "I'm feeling tired. I want to go back. Monro will walk me to Davison."

I had the bitter taste in my mouth again, but without the alcohol to accompany it.

"Please stay," I said. If Veronica left early, people would think it was because she thought the party was bad. "Stay for a dance. I'll change the music to something better. More dancey. You'll forget you're tired. Give me a moment."

I chose the first thing I came to with an insistent beat. A few people migrated in from the garden. "Come on," I called. If Monro danced, it would all be OK.

Hugo was in the living room, swaying and drunk. I heard him say, "Dance with me, Kate. You look bloody gorgeous."

I didn't want to look at him. I only wanted to look at Monro, who was walking towards my outstretched arms. For a second I thought it would be brilliant. We'd dance so our bodies touched, and it would be the beginning of him and me together.

But he did a sidestep while still holding my hands, like a peculiar country-dancing move, and said, "Thanks, Kate. It was a very cool night," and let go.

"Come back after you've walked Veronica home," I said. "There's going to be fireworks soon." I looked at the huge clock above the fireplace. "At midnight. Not long."

Outside I could hear a group joining in with the lyrics, not quite in time.

"I'd like to, but. . ." He was awkward. He didn't know how to tell me he wasn't going to come back, but I knew from his body language, the sunken shoulders and empty stretched-out hands which hung too loosely by his side. "Vee's waiting for me," he said, and he leaned down and kissed me on my cheek, as if I was a relative. "Bye, Kate."

CHAPTER 19

Everything became flat after that. All I wanted was Monro to be there. I admitted it to myself: I'd never felt like this about anyone else. I watched Lo teach Meribel a dance, and I didn't have the energy to join in. I picked up another abandoned glass of pale alcohol and necked it back, and dodged Hugo who kept going on about only wanting one dance. I tried not to think about Monro and Veronica's over-dependent friendship, which had frozen me out tonight. I set about picking up empty glasses and abandoned rubbish. I wanted to be occupied. I took more toilet rolls upstairs to the en-suite bathrooms, and I remembered Veronica's suitcase. I kicked off my shoes and knelt to look under the bed; it was gone.

I stood up and saw Bernard. At least it wasn't Hugo. "Checking Veronica remembered her suitcase," I said because I had to explain the kneeling.

"The hostess with the mostest," he said.

"Yes, that's me," I said, smiling with a light-heartedness I didn't feel. "The party seems to be going well."

"Very well," Bernard said. "I've been running around like a mad thing, keeping an eye on things."

"Thanks," I said. "I'll send everyone through to the garden for the fireworks in a minute."

He caught my arm. "I thought you might want to thank me properly."

I lurched, in my brain and in my body: a synchronized warning.

"A little kiss?" His hand moved to my backside.

I shook his hand off.

He pushed his leg back so the door shut. Not violently. There was no slam. "Don't look so worried."

His words said one thing, but my body was telling me something different. There was too much breath in my throat. Sweat pooled in my armpits.

It was too late to leave the room.

"It's not my fault you're so goddam hot..." said Bernard. He made a grunting noise.

I walked backwards. Soon I'd hit the edge of the bed and my legs would crumple, and I couldn't let that happen. "The fireworks," I said.

"Don't worry about those. I've asked someone else to light them. I've set everything up."

"Let's go and watch them," I said. Bernard was supposed to be my friend. "Please. We have to see the fireworks."

"We might be able to see them from here," said Bernard. He glanced at the window, and then made a sudden grab at my shoulders and his hard mouth pressed on top of mine and his knee pushed between my thighs. I fought to stay upright. There was pain as my lips were rammed against my teeth and his fingers dug into my shoulders, but that was secondary to the scorching fear in my stomach.

I jumped at a whine and whoosh outside. They were followed by the bang of the firework exploding, and the fizzing of sparks as they rained down. Through the window the pink, green and gold blazing chemicals looked like crazed confetti. Bernard moved his hands to my chest.

His mouth was still on mine. Fireworks screamed instead of me.

"Kate?" Meribel's voice was far away. She was shouting something about how I was missing the fireworks.

The door flew open. "Kate?"

Bernard was momentarily distracted, and I moved my face away, and locked eyes with Meribel. Within an instant she was there, pulling me away from Bernard.

"What are you doing?" said Bernard. He wiped his mouth with back of his hand. "Talk about ruining a moment."

Meribel swore at him. I stayed close to her and kept walking out of the room. She slammed the door behind us. "You OK?"

I nodded. I couldn't speak.

Meribel hugged me tight and I was too numb to cry, unable to articulate my gratitude. She led me downstairs into the living room. It was empty because of the fireworks, which were still hissing and whining.

We sat on a sofa together, and she said, "A photographer did the same to me in the summer. Thank God his assistant came in and he stopped. Until then I had thought he was one of the nice ones."

I heard the rest of her words, about how she told her agent and her agent said she'd make sure Meribel never worked with the photographer again, but if she told her parents, they'd make her stop modelling. The other half of my brain was thinking over what just happened. Had I really been in danger, or had I imagined it?

"You'll be all right, Kate," said Meribel, and I realized I was crying. "Do you want me to take you back to Pankhurst?"

I shook my head. I wanted to be where there were lots of people.

Lo appeared on the other side of me, demanding to know where I'd been and why I was crying, and as soon as Meribel said "Get rid of Bernard", Lo disappeared and there was a shouting match in the hall, between her and Bernard, Bernard saying that I was a slag and had she seen me trying to grind with the Mad Dog, and how she of all people had the nerve to have a go at him, he didn't know, and she said, what the hell did that mean. I'd never heard Lo shout like that, in full-on, lose-it fashion.

Some people shot into the living room to see what was going on. Everyone loved a drama. The front door slammed, and Lo came back, flushed, telling us he'd gone.

When I thanked her she said there was nothing to thank her for, and that she was so angry she wanted to kick something. She paced up and down the room then sat with us on the sofa, her head on my shoulder, and said the party was great apart from Bernard, and Sasha not turning up. I ruffled her messy bun, making it even messier, and said it wasn't a party I'd forget in a hurry either.

Outside, people hooked up with each other, and upstairs too for all I knew. Someone reported that Paige and Rob, the bouncer, were horizontal on the garden bench.

Time drifted. It turned into that phase of the party where people either got hyper or chilled, and after a bit, the hyper people started going off to paddle in the sea in dribs and drabs.

By then the music was on low – we didn't want to draw too much attention to ourselves – and I remembered closing my eyes, warm and safe between Meribel and Lo. At first I thought I'd slipped into a nightmare when I heard the shouts and screams.

I was aware of warmth leaving me and I opened my

eyes to see Meribel and Lo run into the garden. My shoes were upstairs but I didn't want to go back into the bedroom to get them, and anyway they were heels, so I went barefooted over sticky floors into the garden.

"Something's happened," said Meribel. She climbed over the low fence and on to the coastal path, where Lo was already running towards the steps which led down to the beach. I looked back at the house. I didn't know who was still in it, if I should abandon it.

Another scream pierced something inside us, and we ran, the three of us to the steps. A boy in our year was running up them. His chest was heaving and he gasped as he was near the top. "We need help. It's Clemmie. She's fallen."

CHAPTER 20

Elsie Gran arrived around eleven-thirty the next morning. I hugged her in the hallway and she took my face in her hands and said, "Are you OK, Katelyn?" and I nodded, because people were watching, but inside I was howling, "NO!"

Clemmie was dead.

We sat with Miss Sneller, the head, and Calding in the junior common room – closed to students for the morning – and Miss Sneller told Elsie Gran how appallingly irresponsible I'd been. "This is a deeply serious matter, Kate," said Miss Sneller. "You will be suspended for one week. As more information comes to light, we will review disciplinary actions. Is there anything you would like to add, Miss Calding?"

Calding shook her head, and said, "We'll talk in a week, Kate."

We were joined by a female police officer who told me to call her Joanna, and there was a discussion about whether we wanted a solicitor present. Elsie Gran said we should just get on with it. Miss Sneller and Calding left, and Joanna said I needed to start at the beginning. She switched on her recording device and asked me how I'd planned the party, and when I told them Steve had booked the rental property for me, Elsie Gran raised her eyes and said, "God help us."

I answered questions about the party, in a steady voice for the first few minutes, and then tearfully, about how much I thought Clemmie had drunk, what time I thought she'd arrived, who she'd spoken to, her argument with Veronica and what I knew about her association with Kipper.

"Did Clemmie have any enemies?" asked Joanna in the same relaxed way she'd asked all the other questions.

I reached for tissues from Elsie Gran and blew my nose. Other girls would probably give my name if they were asked the same question, so I said, "The two of us didn't get on but I wouldn't say we were enemies."

"Why didn't you get on?" asked Joanna.

"We were very different sorts of people," I replied.

At breakfast we'd heard via the Ghost that Kipper had been arrested and held overnight. Some people thought Clemmie might have decided to walk back to Pankhurst, stopped to take a selfie at the gap in the bushes and trees, and slipped. Paige said she must have been the last person to see Clemmie alive. She hadn't seen her go because she'd been with Rob, but she'd heard Clemmie arguing again with Veronica in the distance. She couldn't hear what it was about, but Veronica had been shouting.

It was horrible to think most of us had probably heard Clemmie's scream as she fell, but had mistaken it for a paddler going into the freezing water, somebody's dress getting soaked, or the general drunken end-of-party mayhem. It was some time before Flo and a boy had walked back towards the cliffs to be in the shadows together and discovered her body. That's when the really hysterical screaming had begun.

Joanna asked me to tell her what had happened when Meribel, Lo and I had reached the bottom of the steps, and I told her we'd run to where we saw everyone standing. People were crying, and some were being sick.

"Clemmie's body was sprawled across the rocks. On her front." I took a couple of deep breaths before continuing. "Her dress was all rucked up, and there was blood." My voice cracked and I couldn't speak for a moment because of my shuddery crying. "There was so much blood," I wept. "Her lower body was red. Her arms were like this." I tried to show the improbable angles with my own limbs, and Joanna described them for the recording. I put my head in my hands. "We knew we couldn't do anything. We knew she was dead."

"Did you see anyone move Clemmie's body?" asked Joanna.

"No," I said. I unpeeled my hands to look at her. She would have understood if she'd been there. Nobody wanted to touch the body. It had been horrifying.

Elsie Gran told Joanna to give me a moment, and I sobbed against her as she held me gently. I thought of the photo I'd deleted from my phone after the groyne walk on the first evening of term. It had been of me and Elsie Gran when I was around four. We were sitting on the wall outside her house in the sunshine. She had her arm round me and I was leaning against her, looking up at her and grinning happily, unaware that my face was so odd-looking. She'd always had my back.

Joanna asked if I was ready to continue, and I described how Mount Norton staff had come sprinting along the beach, and had told us to leave and go back to our boarding houses, but we'd been reluctant. We wanted to wait until we saw the police and paramedics. I listed all the staff who were there, including Miss Sneller and the Furball, who were fully dressed, and Calding, who had a navy puffa jacket over her pyjamas.

"It was a bit chaotic," I said. Calding had been hopeless. She had had to be comforted by the Furball. The Ghost had come puffing along the beach from her home, and it had been her who'd rounded up the Pankhurst girls and marched us back.

I had asked Lo and Meribel to sleep in my bed with me because I hadn't wanted to be alone, and we had slept badly, waking up periodically for one of us to say *I can't believe Clemmie's dead*. Our biggest emotion was disbelief, and however much we'd disliked her, we hadn't wished her dead.

Everybody had been at breakfast, including the Davison girls. There was comfort in being with other people, and we had wanted to know what had happened overnight. Calding, solemn and trembling, had made the announcement that Clemmie had died, but there can't have been anybody who didn't already know the news. As girls cried around me, I had cried too, not just because Clemmie was dead; it was hard to have so many accusing eyes upon me too, as if it was my fault for having the party.

What we hadn't known until Calding had announced it was that Veronica and Monro were missing. I hadn't thought to look for Veronica among the huddle of sixth-formers drinking tea and talking in low voices. I'd walked across the car park in a daze last night, and hadn't noticed Monro's car had gone. As soon as Calding told us, I'd thought of Veronica's suitcase, and Monro's nervous behaviour and how now I thought about it, he hadn't been drinking alcohol. He'd even hesitated a moment when I'd first told him the date of the party. It had been planned. His betrayal thudded in my stomach.

When Elsie Gran tapped my knee, I knew I'd lost concentration, and hadn't replied to Joanna's latest question. She asked it again: did I know if Monro and Veronica were going to run away that evening? I replied with an emphatic no.

At the end of the interview, the Ghost knocked on the door, and said she had my parents on the phone. I'd been trying to reach them since early in the morning. She handed me the cordless office phone, and said I could take it in the office for privacy.

I stood by the office window looking down the empty road before I said hello. You could see all the way to the end in the direction we walked to and from school.

"Hello, Kate," came the deep voice of my father. "Having a tricky time, hmm?" He asked me what he needed to do to fix the situation.

"There isn't anything," I said. I told him about finding Clemmie dead on the rocks, about the shock of it, the blood, how her body had basically broken in a thousand places. He made hmmming noises, and said it sounded as if I needed some rest, and a week's suspension should help with that. He didn't ask anything about the party, and that was fine by me. I wondered what he'd say if I told him about Bernard. I'd done my best to block out that part of the party, but now I had to lean against the window because I was worried my knees might give way with the what ifs. I couldn't imagine putting what had happened into words.

By the time my father handed me over to my mother I was quiet-crying, and she didn't like it when I cried. She asked if they should be looking for another school for me, talking over my tears. If it had been any other week, she'd have suggested I fly over and be with them, but the new clinic was taking all their time, and it was stressful. I was better off with Elsie Gran. And crying wasn't going to help anybody.

I'd hardly ever seen her cry herself. I once said that to Elsie Gran while she was weeping at a police drama on TV, and she said my mother had had so much plastic surgery her tear ducts had probably been removed.

When the call was over, I was given half an hour to pack a bag. I thought of Sasha doing the same thing last term. She'd been asked to leave during the school day. The things she hadn't managed to pack were sent on afterwards.

As it was a Sunday, I got the chance to say goodbye to Meribel and Lo. They came into my room, and sat on my bed, and told me it wasn't my fault Clemmie died. I hadn't been responsible for her. They said they'd message me if Elsie Gran didn't take my phone away, and I assured them that was unlikely.

I walked down the two flights of stairs like a disgraced celebrity. Girls came out of their rooms to stare or say goodbye. Zeta stood on the first floor landing clutching her hamster cushion to her stomach. "You'll be OK," she whispered as I went by. Knowing Zeta felt sorry for me made me feel one hundred times worse.

Elsie Gran drove by the sea. The police were still there. The car park and coastal path were cordoned off. A small group of locals were hanging around trying to see what was going on, and there was a lone reporter and camera person. For once, Elsie Gran didn't put on an audiobook thriller and we went home in silence.

A couple of hours later, Bel and Lo messaged to say Kipper had been released without charge. Someone had overheard the Ghost tell Squirrel there was insufficient evidence.

For the rest of the day and the next, I lay on my bed in my room with the windows that needed fixing, and the once-white, scruffy walls that were stained where I'd accidentally sprayed it with Diet Coke a few summers ago when Josie, my only friend in the area, came over. She was Maria-from-next-door's granddaughter, and was probably the only person in the world apart from Maria and me who properly understood Elsie Gran, which meant I never had to explain away her eccentricities.

I'd been given a hastily put together folder of work to do while I was suspended, but I was in no rush to tackle it yet. I sketched hands in an old notebook, thought constantly of Clemmie stepping back into nothing and the terror she must have felt as she fell, and messaged back and forth with Meribel and Lo. They told me Clemmie's parents had arrived at Pankhurst, and Veronica's had been spotted going into Davison. There were police and other officials coming and going.

When Elsie Gran came back from the allotment with runner beans and odd-shaped potatoes, I said I wanted to paint my bedroom. Until now I'd quite liked its scruffiness. It was a nice contrast to my bedroom in

Dubai, which was more like a hotel room. After assuring her I wasn't expecting her to pay for it, she drove me to the DIY store where I chose pineapple-yellow paint, a roller, paint tray, brushes and masking tape.

As my room became brighter, I went over and over the same two thoughts.

First: it was hard to imagine that Clemmie had drunkenly taken a selfie and slipped, but it was even harder to imagine the alternative, which was that someone had pushed her. The people with the opportunity to do it were anyone going down to the beach, and those who'd already left the party: Kipper, Bernard, Monro and Veronica.

Second: why had Monro and Veronica run away together? Was their disappearance really linked to Clemmie's death? If the two of them had been planning to run away for some time, had they also been planning to attack Clemmie?

I sat on the top of the stepladder holding the paint tray in my lap and thought about the kiss I'd shared with Monro before the party started. He'd known then he'd be leaving later with Veronica. Had any part of him wanted to tell me, or was he just keeping himself occupied until he left? If I closed my eyes, I could conjure up the feeling of swelling pleasure ... until it was tainted by a sense of dread and panic, and I remembered Bernard's grunting face. I opened my eyes and stood up again to keep painting. I did that section twice. It had to be thorough.

I slept on a mattress in Elsie Gran's cluttered study that night because I hadn't finished painting. It was the room my father had slept in when he was little. My father studied hard. He went to medical school. He became a plastic surgeon, initially what Elsie Gran called the right sort. He helped patients with disfigurements as a result of birth defects, accidents or disease. He crossed into different territory when he met my mother, an actress in a popular Brazilian soap opera. By the time she'd been given the part, she'd already had quite a few surgeries.

I once tried to tell Elsie Gran my mother had made certain decisions about her looks because she'd been born poor and wanted to make money, but Elsie Gran said that was absolutely no excuse. She never had a good word to say about her.

Thinking about my father made me want to search out the family photo albums in the untidy cupboard in the corner. There weren't many of them. Elsie Gran stopped putting photos in albums when her camera broke several years ago, and she didn't bother printing any from her phone. I hardly ever looked through them. The photo I'd had on my phone had been loose on her desk. There were a few small blurry photos of family get-togethers when Elsie Gran was a child, black and white photos of her as an art student and peace activist in the Sixties, lots of my father when he was a solemn toddler through to a straggly haired hippy kid, and then a teenager with unruly hair, holding a hand up to say he didn't want to be photographed.

The reason his hair was like that was because of his ears. He hated how they stuck out, and as soon as he could afford to do it, he had them pinned, then his hair cut short.

In the photos of me as a toddler, I had the same dark, serious eyes and similar ears, which looked like pull-here-to-open tabs. I closed the album and put it down the side of my bed, but my head still played the conversation I overheard my parents having as they looked at pictures of me taken on my sixth birthday. My ears needed pinning and my nose needed straightening. My droopy eyelid was getting worse, and there was something not quite right about my chin.

I wasn't nice to look at.

My ears were fixed when I was six and a half. When I was thirteen, I had a nose job, chin implant and an eyelid lift, carried out by a top plastic surgeon in the States, a friend of my father's. Elsie Gran said it should have been against the law to have it done so young, but it wasn't. Not for someone who had connections and could travel. And at that age I wanted it done so badly.

I wanted to be perfect.

CHAPTER 21

It took me a full two days to paint my bedroom. I kept stopping to hear the latest from Bel and Lo, either by message or FaceTime. Clemmie's laptop and other electronic devices had been taken away by the police. Monro and Veronica were still missing, though everyone said they'd be found any moment. All it would take was for Monro's car number plate to go through the right CCTV cameras.

Meribel said she'd reported walking in on Bernard assaulting me, and Miss Sneller said she'd look into it, and hadn't Bernard and I been a couple at one point? She was sure somebody had told her that.

I shook my head at this, but let them continue.

Lo said Bernard was telling people he'd left the party early because of a row with me over the fireworks. He'd been heard saying Monro and Veronica leaving the beach house fitted with the time Clemmie had been thought to wander off, and everyone knew Monro had difficulty controlling himself. It was well-known Monro was very protective of Veronica, and there was bad feeling between Clemmie and Veronica.

I sucked in my breath angrily. "That's—" I began, but the two of them had something else to say.

"Guess what?" said Meribel. She turned to Lo. They were back from school, sitting side by side on Lo's bed, with Meribel's pale grey cashmere wrap round both of them. It gave me a pang of missing out.

"We've found out *why* there was bad feeling between them," said Lo.

Beside her, Meribel nodded vigorously, desperate to tell me.

"Hugo eventually told a girl in my chemistry class, who told me," said Meribel. "Clemmie's dad has a gambling problem and he lost all their money. Veronica's parents lent him more to help them, but he gambled that too. Apparently Clemmie's dad's recently filed for bankruptcy and that's why she went mad about RapBros."

"RapBros didn't go bankrupt because of gambling though," I said.

"But they still went bankrupt," said Meribel. "I feel bad now."

"She hadn't even told Paige," said Lo.

Meribel pulled her portion of the wrap further up her shoulder. "Rumour is that Clemmie was going to have to leave Mount Norton if she didn't get a scholarship."

They were focused on me now, as I realized the significance of what Meribel had just said. The exam paper that was found under Sasha's mattress was a scholarship paper. There were different types of scholarship at Mount Norton, worth varying percentages of the fees. Some were annual scholarships; others lasted from the first to the end of the fifth form. Sasha usually sat annual scholarships to top up her sports scholarship. Nobody would have thought for a minute Clemmie would be sitting for an annual scholarship.

"Do you think there's any chance Clemmie slipped out at some point, while you were working on your assignment together?" asked Lo.

Say it. Tell them.

"The two of us were saying Clemmie might have tampered with her own light switch so her parents could sue the school and get money for fees," said Meribel.

"What d'you think of our theory?" asked Lo.

I stopped chewing my bottom lip. "It's quite extreme. I'm not sure Clemmie knew enough about electricity."

"We're keeping that one to ourselves for now," said Lo. She gave Meribel a look to confirm what she was saying. "Nobody wants to hear anything bad about her right now."

The dinner bell rang and Meribel said, "We'd better go."

Lo was already off the bed, out of shot, but then her head came into view again. "I forgot to tell you the strangest thing that happened today." They were talking to me as they went down the stairs with Meribel's phone. "We went to Davison," continued Lo, "and on Veronica's collage there was a printout about a hospital in America. Like, who would put that up there after what's happened? When Clemmie's dead and Veronica's run away?"

"A hospital in America," I said slowly.

"Yeah, a fancy one in Florida with a name like ... like a theme park or something." Lo shrugged. "We have to say goodbye now. Speak to you tomorrow. Love you!"

The two of them blew kisses and were gone.

That artwork... *The things we keep hidden.*

Amber Park Hospital, Florida, was where I'd had my plastic surgery. How had anybody found that out? Who had Clemmie told about my plastic surgery, and why did they think *now* was a good time to unnerve me?

After painting my bedroom, it took me another day to rearrange my furniture, reposition my posters, and hang up a mirror that Elsie Gran had found in a skip down the road when some neighbours had their extension built. I stared into the mirror, at my ears, eyes, chin and nose, and at my skin, with its peculiar tint from the light bouncing off the Pineapple Yellow walls. I took the mirror down and placed it in the gap between the wall and my chest of drawers.

I wondered if anyone had hacked into my hospital files, or been in contact with my parents. How much had Clemmie told Paige? The thought of the photo of Amber Park Hospital on Veronica's artwork kept coming back to me.

The following day, I wrote two essays, filled in a maths worksheet, and mixed jars of paint for the different skin tones of Elsie Gran's hands, which I'd take back to school for my paper-clay version.

I matched them against her hands as she was doing the crossword in an old newspaper of Maria's.

After I was satisfied with my range of colours, she said, "Come with me to the allotment. We need some carrots."

"Isn't it raining?" I said.

She pushed her glasses up on to her head and said, "It's only drizzle."

We had barely spoken about the reason for my suspension. Elsie Gran only knew what she'd heard me tell Joanna, the police officer. I thought she was waiting for me to start the conversation, and I wasn't keen to have it. But as we walked along together under a big umbrella she said, "You had the party because you wanted it, did you, Katelyn? You weren't pressurized because you're head Pankhurst person?"

"House Prefect," I corrected. "Yes, I wanted to have the party." It was ninety-nine per cent true. There was no point telling her about the tradition of the House Prefect organizing a party and the rules around it. She'd have said that was ridiculous. It was OK for her. She enjoyed doing things differently to everyone else.

She nodded.

I didn't say anything. Sometimes her views on life could tip into rants, and I wasn't up for that at the moment.

At the allotment, we pulled carrots out of the soft ground, and we gathered big windfall apples, turning them over to check they weren't rotten before placing them in a shopping bag. When the rain came down more heavily we retreated to the wooden shed, and sat on deckchairs with the door open. I told her it was like being in a beach hut and she laughed, and got up to see if there were any biscuits in the tin she kept on the top shelf. There were her usual plain ones, soft and almost tasteless from being in the tin so long, but we ate two each and Elsie Gran said she wished she'd had the sense to bring a thermos of tea. That made me think of Monro, and I hadn't been thinking about him for at least thirty minutes.

The rain stopped and so did our conversation. It was only as Elsie Gran was turning the combination on the padlock for the shed door that she said, "Unspeakable things happened at my school. Maybe they did for your father too. He didn't tell me much."

I nodded, to show I'd heard. I felt a rush of wanting to tell her about Bernard. His cheery face, vaguely comical name, and his sexual innuendo. The ease with which he pushed himself on me, and his gropey-fingered, slug-tongued entitlement. My stomach turned inside out at the memory of the humiliation, and the shame I felt for not biting or scratching him. For not finding the strength to break away and shout. For having to be rescued by Bel. For only being rescued by luck.

The shame was bigger than the sudden desire to tell her.

"There are other schools you can go to," said Elsie Gran. She tugged at the padlock to check it was locked.

"That's what Mama said." I shook the umbrella so the raindrops flew off.

"Really?" Elsie Gran was surprised. "I meant schools round here. She probably didn't."

"I like Mount Norton though," I said. "I couldn't leave my friends." The thought of starting at a new school, after all I had achieved, made me ill. It was Friday already. After the weekend, I'd be back there.

Elsie Gran made a *huh* noise, which could have meant anything.

Back home, I was kept busy peeling carrots and apples, and Elsie Gran looked up a recipe for apple brandy.

I went to bed early in my yellow room, and waited for updates from Bel and Lo.

They FaceTimed to say a memorial concert was being planned for Clemmie. They hadn't seen much of Calding. She'd either been in her office having meetings with hysterical parents, in meetings at the main school with Miss Sneller, or absent entirely.

Lo said I should look up Clemmie's death online. The two of them waited while I logged on to my laptop. It had made a couple of newspapers, and several online articles. Miss Sneller was quoted as saying there'd been a recent change of housemistress at Pankhurst, and accusations that the housemistress Ms Scarlet Calding was too inexperienced were untrue, but the school would be reviewing her position and the procedures of Mount Norton boarding houses.

"She'll probably sack Calding to please the parents," said Meribel. "Which would obviously be a good thing. Can't happen soon enough."

"Depending who we get next," said Lo, and she played me a new track she'd discovered by an upcoming K-pop band.

After we'd said goodnight, we still kept messaging back and forth.

Lo said the Ghost and the Furball had taken on extra hours to provide so-called support, but that support mostly meant setting up movies and making sure no one left Pankhurst unless they were supposed to. There was talk of a counsellor being brought in.

People were starting to recast Clemmie as a universally adored student. A donation site had been set up. Some students were lobbying for a stained-glass window in the assembly hall to commemorate her life. Paige wanted a prize in Clemmie's name at Founders Day for the student who had demonstrated the most school spirit throughout the year.

Bel said Bernard had thrown a book at someone in the Davison common room for saying they'd heard he was chucked out of the party for trying it on with me.

The book. Monro had folded over a page with a map.

Was that a book on hidden treasures? I messaged. *Did he find it under a chair?*

The others found the question hilarious and asked why I wanted to know. I told them it was Monro's and before he ran away he was looking for it and I said I'd keep an eye out for it, so could they retrieve it for me. I still hadn't told the two of them about my kiss with Monro. I didn't want it analysed and to open a big enquiry about why he hadn't told me anything about running away with Veronica. Or why I had such a bad track record with guys.

Monro didn't have Instagram, but Veronica did. I didn't think for one second she'd post where she and Monro were, but I thought there might be other leads. The last thing she'd posted was the Polaroid-style photo of her and Monro on top of the café, the image on her original artwork. It was different in style from her other photos, which seemed to be close-up shots of paint and beads and anything art-related. I read her bio. *Sixth-former. Feminist. Campaigner. Art startler. New art project coming soon.* There was a website address which I clicked on, but it took me to a this-website-is-still-a-work-in-progress message.

I placed my phone on the floor, and turned on to my side to go to sleep. I couldn't imagine going to a local school like Josie, Maria's granddaughter. She said her nan thought my parents were stuck-up idiots, but according to her nan I wasn't a lost cause yet. A few times Josie had invited me out with her and her friends but I'd made excuses. I liked her, but she knew me before my plastic surgery, and it made me anxious to think what she might have told her friends about me.

My phone pinged. I fished for it on the floor, and read the screen. There was a message from Lo.

It said, *I've found Sasha.*

CHAPTER 22

The blood in my veins faltered. I waited to see if Lo would add anything else. I couldn't bring myself to ask, but I needed more information.

Another message beeped. *She's in intensive care. In a medically induced coma. There was an accident five weeks ago.*

This was so far from what I was expecting, I said "What?" out loud. My fingers were desperate to message now. I typed, *How do you know?*

Lo started to type, sending a sentence at a time:

Internet search.

I've done it before but her name came up this time.

A road traffic accident.

Someone wrote about it on a community website.

Some people are trying to get a pedestrian crossing put in because she was the second person to be hit by a car at the same place.

She was waiting for me to chip in with something.

That's terrible, I finally messaged. I'd thought Sasha's life would be OK after Mount Norton. She was so clever, so full of everything that should have propelled her forward. I felt irrationally angry with her about the accident.

Lo replied: *If it's medically induced I think there's more likelihood of her being OK?*

I trembled as I replied. *Honestly? I don't know.*

Lo kept going.

I found out the name of the hospital.

Called them up already.

They said she can't have visitors apart from family.

But I'm going anyway.

I'm going to take a card for when she wakes up.

Bel says I shouldn't do it.

I tap out, *Maybe Bel's right.* I think about deleting the *maybe*, but send it. There's a long pause during which Lo's hurt transports itself telepathically, before she resumes.

I've looked up trains.

It takes forty-five minutes from your gran's.

I don't want to go on my own.

Will you come with me?

Tomorrow.

Bel won't come.

Please?

194

Tomorrow was Saturday, and it would be easy for Lo to leave school for the day if she could fake parental permission. Elsie Gran would be fine with me going; she never stopped me going anywhere, but she had rules about what time I needed to be home. Lo knew how relaxed she was.

OK, I message back. *Let's make a plan in the morning.* I'd go with her, out of guilt. I owed both of them.

Lo replied immediately. *THANK YOU. LY* ♥

I felt sick.

I remembered everything before I even opened my eyes in the morning. Today I was going with Lo to deliver a card to a girl in a coma I should have saved from expulsion.

I picked up my phone – Lo had sent through an itinerary, complete with a meeting place at Thornbury station. I had a shower, taking so long that Elsie Gran banged on the door and told me to consider the planet, and dressed in my most ordinary clothes. I didn't want to stand out today.

I told Elsie Gran I was off to meet Lo for the day. She was listening to one of her thrillers on audiobook in the kitchen, so she nodded, checked I had my phone and waved me away. She didn't know my Mount Norton friends, other than to say hello to them when she dropped me off or picked me up.

The train was slow, stopping at every single station along the track to Thornbury. At each one, I felt the urge to get out and run away from what was ahead. It made me think of Monro and Veronica. Monro was so frequently in my thoughts these days, I'd almost become used to the ache of not knowing why he'd left, and of missing him. If he were here now, next to me, I'd shift across the seat so our bodies would touch. I'd reach for his hand, and he'd clasp it tight, and he would keep holding it as I would explain why I lied and told everyone that Clemmie was in my bedroom doing our geography project when she hadn't been.

There was a small part of me too which couldn't help wondering if he'd been caught up in Clemmie's death somehow. I'd kept secrets from him, and I wasn't stupid enough to think he hadn't kept any from me.

Lo met me on the platform. Her face was serious, scanning the passengers' faces, but when she saw me it widened into happiness. I waved and grinned back, and then I was on the platform, and we hugged. She told me she was grateful I'd come, and my gut felt so twisted it hurt.

"I've scoped it out," said Lo. "We'll get the bus. It's too far to walk." She placed her hands on her temples. "Oh, God. This is so awful. But it explains why Sasha wasn't in touch about the party, doesn't it?"

I nodded, aware my mouth was lacking its usual amount of saliva. We'd walked out of the station, Lo leading the way to the bus stop.

There was hardly a pause in her conversation. She

told me how claustrophobic Pankhurst had become, with the favourite topics of conversation being why and how Clemmie had fallen, Veronica and Monro's disappearance, and my suspension. Most people thought Kipper had pushed Clemmie and got away with it because of the lack of evidence. Anyone who'd been identified as having been at my illegal party wasn't allowed out of their boarding houses past seven p.m. until the end of term as a punishment. Journalists had been stopping to talk to anyone in Mount Norton uniform but Miss Sneller had banned anyone from speaking to them. All the time she was speaking, Lo bent her fingers back nervously.

"I don't want to bump into Sasha's family," she said, as we stepped down from the bus when it stopped in front of the sprawling hospital. "It would be too weird."

I was finding it hard to walk, my leg muscles felt weak.

There was an information desk in the hospital's main entrance, but we were intercepted by a grey-haired lady with a sash that read *I'm Here To Help* as we made our way towards it. She told us where to find the intensive care unit, and said, "All the best, darling," when Lo thanked her.

My dread ascended in the lift with us. It was crowded, but nobody spoke apart from a couple at the back who were murmuring. Lo and I were the only ones to get off at the fourth floor, emerging into a white world of corridors. It smelled of cleaning products, underpinned by smells too worrying to contemplate. The signage to the intensive care unit was large and unmistakeable. Lo unbuckled her bag and pulled out an envelope. She'd drawn an anime character in one corner, and Sasha's name in super-fine pen.

We went through a set of double doors, but needed to press a buzzer to get through the next set. Lo looked at me for reassurance and I nodded faintly. She pressed it firmly but nobody came. We gave it a couple more minutes, then Lo pressed again.

The double doors behind us squeaked as they opened and a nurse came towards us. "Can I help?" he asked briskly, as if he was in a hurry. "You have a family member in here?"

"No," I said quickly, before Lo was tempted to lie. "We're friends."

Lo shot me an angry look and said, "We, er ... we're friends of Sasha Mires. I have a card for her." She held it up.

The nurse scrunched one side of his face trying to recall her. "Sasha, Sasha... Ah, yes, I can take that for you. No problem." He took it and was gone.

"You ruined it, Kate," said Lo. She leaned against the closed door. "We might have at least got the other side of this door if you hadn't said that. I'd have done anything just to have seen her."

"I didn't think," I said. "I'm sorry." It scared me to think we might bump into Sasha's family at any moment. "The nurse would have checked us out. We'd have been made to wait and then it would have been embarrassing when they said they knew we were lying. Come on. Let's get out of here. I don't like hospitals."

Lo sighed and pushed against the door as she stood straight. "I can't believe Sasha's the other side of here," she said.

I set off down the corridor, and let her catch me up. "Let's get something to eat in that shop near the information desk and go outside," I said.

The small shop was massively overpriced, but we bought juice and a couple of brittle-looking cookies, individually wrapped. There were benches at the front of the hospital, overlooking the main road and car park, designed perhaps to keep people from lingering too long. There was only one free one and we ran to get it before anyone else did, which meant Lo was laughing as she sat down. She took a long sip from her juice carton. The straw was in her mouth for the longest time, but when I glanced at her, I saw she wasn't drinking; she was staring at a couple who were making their way to the hospital entrance. There was no mistaking it was Sasha's parents, but her father was stooped and her mother was moving slowly. They'd become old.

Lo pulled the straw from her mouth. "It's them, isn't it?"

"Yes." We watched them disappear from sight, and Lo sighed, as if she'd been thinking of running over to them but decided not to. I broke my cookie into pieces while it was still in its cellophane wrapping, and then into dusty crumbs. "I've got something to tell you," I said.

Lo looked at my cookie. "What's the matter?"

It felt like stepping off a cliff. "I know it wasn't Sasha's fault. Her being expelled."

"How?" asked Lo in a quiet voice.

"Clemmie never came to our room," I said. I closed my eyes for a fraction of a second. I was in free fall, Lo's revulsion rushing up to meet me. "She made me say she had."

"Why would you cover for her?" asked Lo, a groove of a frown deep in her forehead. She was trying to understand this.

I looked at her and winced. "I'm so sorry," I said. "Clemmie told me if I didn't cover for her she'd post a photo of me online."

"What photo?" asked Lo.

I told her about the plastic surgery, how I hated how I'd looked before, and the horror I'd felt when I realized Clemmie had somehow found out about it. I explained how panicked I was to think she had a photo of me. There had been photos taken at some of the other schools I'd been to when I hadn't been quick enough to dodge them, but I hadn't thought they would resurface.

"I didn't want anyone to know," I said. How could I tell her at Mount Norton I was finally somebody special, and I was desperate not to lose that?

"You lied for Clemmie because you were worried we'd

see what you looked like before you had plastic surgery?"
Lo's voice was tight. She stood up. "Sasha was expelled for
something she didn't do and you let it happen because you
had *plastic surgery*?" I could tell she was imagining how I
looked before the operations. There were tears in her eyes.
"You let me believe my girlfriend was a cheat and a liar."

I bit my lip.

"I can't be here with you any more," said Lo. As she
walked away she said, "You disgust me."

CHAPTER 23

On Monday morning, I got dressed in school uniform, without rolling up my skirt, and Elsie Gran drove me back to Mount Norton. Lo hadn't replied to any of my messages, and Bel hadn't been in touch, so I guessed Lo had told her.

Elsie Gran selected an audiobook for the journey and we listened in horror as a character was pushed off a tower block. She switched it off mid-scream. I had a flashback to Clemmie's body at the bottom of the cliff, twisted and lifeless, and quelled the nausea by opening the car window an inch and breathing in the outside air. "What was the story with your old house mistress? Why was she sacked?" Elsie Gran asked, after a few minutes. "Wibbzie, was that what you called her?"

"*Wibbz*. She showed some parents round Pankhurst while she was drunk. Everyone says there was an email about it. Did you get it?"

"Probably," said Elsie Gran. "They send so many emails. I found her quite a nosy woman. I don't suppose she's any great loss."

"I miss her," I replied. "She was really nice compared to Calding, the new one."

"Hmm. The new lady's quite intense, don't you think?" said Elsie-Gran.

"Totally," I said. "At least she's temporary."

When we sat, an hour later, with Calding in her office, I saw Elsie Gran look round the room while Calding spoke at length about chances and expectations. It was still as bare and impersonal as it had been at the beginning of term.

"How temporary are you, Ms Calding?" asked Elsie Gran, and I boomeranged back into the conversation and cringed.

Calding blinked, and something crossed her face which made her look really young, though when she spoke it was in her stiff voice. "That's still to be decided," she said. "You'll be informed when a replacement is found, and until then please be reassured that I'll be keeping a close eye on your granddaughter."

"This school thinks it's better than it is," said Elsie Gran and I lowered my head in embarrassment.

"I agree," said Calding.

This was so unexpected that Elsie Gran paused before saying, "And the fees are obscenely high. It's my son who pays. I'd never have sent Katelyn here if it had been down to me."

"Please," I said to Elsie Gran, putting my hand on her arm, "stop it." I wanted this all to be over. I wasn't sure I was ready to be back here. I was Kate Lynette Jordan-Ferreira, but Lo wasn't speaking to me, possibly Bel too, and when a couple of third-formers had seen me earlier they'd looked away.

The meeting came to an end, and I said goodbye to Elsie Gran in the hall. There was nothing to suggest that a student had died a week ago. The floor was as polished and the flowers just as vibrant as usual. The rules which Calding had stuck on the wall had been removed, though, with no trace of the Blu-Tack she'd stuck them up with.

"Do your best," said Elsie Gran. "Remember how much I love you." She kissed me on the cheek, and I hugged her hard, inhaling her old-lady perfume, the one I'd only ever smelled on her, and it made me sad because I knew I'd forget the exact smell of it by the time she'd walk down the front steps.

The first person I saw after I said goodbye was Zeta. She came out of the junior common room with a magazine.

"Are you OK?" she asked. She looked different, more relaxed and sure of herself.

"Yes," I said, angry with myself for the tears welling up in my eyes at Elsie Gran going. "You?"

"Good, thanks," she said. "I've got an appointment with the orthodontist. Miss Calding is taking me in about five minutes. Are you sure you're OK?"

I nodded. I picked up my bag, which I'd left in the hall during my meeting with Calding. "Have Veronica and Monro been found?"

Zeta shook her head. "School keeps asking if we've heard from them. Nobody has. There was a reported sighting of them in Birmingham on Twitter, but that was it."

On the top floor the doors to our bedrooms were closed – which was how we always left them when we went to school – but they looked even more unwelcoming today. The cleaners had tidied my room. On my bed was the *Hidden Treasures* book. On top of it was a note from Lo telling me she'd appreciate it if I didn't talk to her about Sasha. I put the note in my bin, then messaged her and Bel to say I was back.

I stood by the window. The sea was dark grey today, cold looking. It hit me, the enormity of what I'd done to Sasha, denying her her rightful place here. Even if she recovered, her injuries were likely to be too severe to ever come back, even if she wanted to. I'd ruined so much for her, including her sporting ambitions, and very probably her chance to go to a top university and have a high-flying career.

I understood now how desperate Clemmie had been

205

to win that scholarship, and for people not to know how dramatically her home circumstances had changed. She'd known way before I did that we hadn't been so dissimilar, me and her. Pankhurst felt disturbingly incomplete with her and Sasha gone.

Calding had told me I had to go to afternoon lessons, but I wouldn't. Not today – not art class. I wasn't willingly going to be in the same room as Bernard. I lay on the bed and flipped through the book. There were several pages with turned-over corners, including the map I'd seen. One of them was a page on art galleries in the Birmingham area. The other six pages were in different parts of the country. I could trace Monro and Veroncia's probable route up to Scotland by the turned-over pages. They might have hidden the car by now, knowing the police would be looking for it.

I opened the window and went on to the fire escape, leaning against the railings to look into Churchill's grounds. Monro should be there on the bench, beckoning me down for a talk, or a trip to throw pebbles into the sea, or a kiss. I turned so that I was leaning against the railings the other way, and I took my phone from my skirt pocket. I'd send him a message.

Hope you're ok. I have your Hidden Treasures book and think you're in Scotland. I won't say anything, don't worry.

After I'd sent it, everything felt normal, as if Monro might text me back. That feeling only lasted a few minutes.

Turned out, I couldn't avoid art. The Ghost glided up

to the top floor and said she was going to accompany me to the main school. She tried to make conversation as we walked, telling me Squirrel had organized two themed dinners the previous week to keep people's spirits up in what she called "this unsettled period". The themes had been American diner and Indian banquet. She proceeded to list the foods she'd liked, and then those she hadn't. Silence would have been preferable.

"There's going to be a school concert in memory of Clemmie," said the Ghost. "Miss Wibberton is going to come. That'll be nice, won't it?"

I nodded. We were nearly at the art room. Panic seized me round the throat and my legs were rubbery. I had an overwhelming desire to sink to the floor and tuck myself into a ball.

The Ghost opened the door and in I went. "Ah, a latecomer," said Mr Hayes. "Very good to see you, Ms Jordan-Ferreira. Your hands sculpture is coming along well. Make sure you get it in the kiln this week."

All eyes were on me. I was an object of curiosity: someone teetering on the edge of a fall from grace. Anybody who hadn't been invited to the party or who resented me in any way would be especially interested in how things would go over the next few weeks.

I sensed Bernard rather than saw him, and headed for the art cupboard to fetch my sculpture, which meant I could keep my back to him. I carried it to my table holding tight to the wooden board it was on, taking care not to look in his direction.

He made me jump when he appeared at my side, and I immediately reached for my ceramics scalpel. It was so sharp it sliced through fresh clay like butter. As I held it, I thought of my father, and other surgeons, cutting through human flesh.

"I think we should clear the air about the party," said Bernard. He gave no indication he was concerned about me wielding the scalpel. "I realize I came on too strong," he said.

You frightened me.

"But we'd made out at the last party and I thought you were up for it."

You knew I wasn't.

"Your friends pissed me right off, if I'm honest, making out that I was some sort of . . . animal. That was really unfair."

Something worse would have happened if Bel hadn't come in.

"I hope we can put this behind us and carry on being friends, yeah?"

I hate you.

"Kate?"

I leaned down to trim the clay hands with the scalpel, despite my own hands shaking ever so slightly.

"God, you're not worth it. I should have let you carry on making a fool of yourself with the Mad Dog. Oh, and where is he now? Run away with the lovely Veronica. What have *they* got to hide, hmm?"

I breathed in sharply. Tears fell on my out-breath, but I

wasn't going to let Bernard see them. I made myself walk slowly to the sink for a paper towel from the dispenser above it, and I went into the cupboard where I could get my breathing under control.

I leaned against a section of empty shelving and blew my nose. Outside I heard Bernard say, "It's OK, sir. She's emotional because it's the first day back after her suspension. It's suddenly hit her, you know, what happened at the party."

CHAPTER 24

I left the art room as soon as I could and waited for Lo and Meribel outside school in our usual place by the bush that was clipped into a spiral shape.

Meribel came out of the main entrance with a group of Churchill boys from our year, and waved me over. We hugged, but Meribel was half-hearted about it. I wanted to tell her what Bernard had said, but the boys were eager to hear how much trouble I was in for having the party, and if I had any news about Monro. They were disappointed with my answers of *I'm not sure*, and *no*. When I didn't start walking down the drive with them, Meribel grabbed my arm. "Come on, Kate."

"What about Lo?" I said.

Meribel shook her head. "Nope. We're not waiting." She moved closer to me, and said, "Lo's taken the Sasha thing hard. Give her some space." She was looking behind me.

I followed her gaze, and saw Lo emerging from a side entrance. She was with one of the scholarship girls from another house. She saw me, stopped dead and turned away quickly.

Meribel still had a hold of my arm, and she pulled me towards the boys, who were laughing about something that had happened in a previous lesson. "Don't. Just don't." She spoke in a low voice so the boys didn't overhear. "You have no idea how upset she was when she came back from that hospital." She appraised my face. "Your plastic surgeon was good."

Instinctively, I covered a hand over my nose and chin.

"I can't imagine my parents letting me have plastic surgery before I was eighteen," said Meribel.

She didn't understand how asymmetrical my face had been – or what my parents were like. I let my hand slide down my nose. I felt the contour of my perfect nose against my fingers, the nose I both loved and hated. "My father arranged it in the States. It was done by a friend of his."

Meribel carried on staring. "You're literally not the person I thought you were." She glanced ahead at the boys. "Lo told Sneller about you giving Clemmie a false alibi. You'll get called in to see her."

My stomach dropped. I knew I'd be called in, but I hadn't wanted to think about the implications. What would happen now I'd been exposed as a liar? Would the police want to re-interview me once they knew I'd held back information? Had I made myself a suspect?

"I'm curious about something," said Meribel, and I braced myself for what was coming. "Did you *want* Sasha to leave? Were you jealous Lo was so into her?"

"Of course not," I said, but there's heat at the back of my neck. It was true; there was something about Sasha that I didn't like. She could be distant, laugh at our dances or roll her eyes at some of our conversations, and say we weren't living in the real world. I was worried she'd suck Lo away. For the first time in my life it had felt as if I *was somebody*, and I *had friends*, and I didn't want to lose them.

We caught up with the boys, and I made appropriate faces at the punchlines to their jokes. It seemed they had bets going of when Monro and Veronica would be found, and quite a lot of money had been lost so far.

As we walked into Pankhurst, everyone stared at me. I was Kate Lynette Jordan-Ferreira, but my reputation had changed. The Pankhurst party had gone badly wrong on my watch. I didn't want tea, cake or conversation, and even though I went straight up to my room, I was still stopped on the stairs by a couple of second-formers coming down. One asked me if Clemmie had been high when she'd fallen off the cliff, and her friend had commented dryly that of course she'd been high: the cliffs were at least thirty metres. I said, "No comment," and darted round them.

I sat on my bed and listened to a playlist of songs by a seventeen-year-old singer from Argentina who Lo, Bel and I had been briefly obsessed with in between our love of everything Korean – and sketched hands in a notebook. I couldn't stop drawing them. Hands revealed a lot about a person. They could give away how that person was thinking, and how old they were. People didn't often think about getting plastic surgery on their hands unless there was a medical reason.

When there was a knock at my door a little while later, I called out, "Come in," expecting it to be Lo or Bel; it was Zeta.

After a nervous hello, she said, "I thought you should know, there's a printout of you on Veronica's artwork, with the word 'fake' across it."

My head thumped with humiliation. News travelled fast. Zeta gazed at me. "I wanted to warn you – so you could act like you didn't care."

I nodded. It was hard to stomach her sympathy. "You've started hanging out at Davison, then?" I said.

"Yes. It's easier without Clemmie," she said.

"How d'you mean?" I asked. I sensed she was trying to tell me something.

Zeta looked at her feet. "She knew about my mum. Clemmie said unless I bought things for her she'd tell everyone about her."

I wanted to know about her mum now, but I knew it wasn't fair to ask. "What things?"

213

"Make-up, skincare, perfumes, clothes. . ."

You're a scholarship kid.

"I couldn't say no." Zeta was clearly hoping I'd understand, and I did. "I couldn't tell my dad. He's so proud of me getting a scholarship here." She gave a tiny shrug of I-had-no-choice.

"How did you afford all those things?" I asked.

"I used my allowance. I stole a few things. I worked in the holidays." Her shoulders dropped. "It's over now."

"Have you told anyone else?" I asked.

"Ms Calding," said Zeta. "I told her today when she took me to the orthodontist. She was really nice about it, but I don't want everyone to know."

"I'm glad you told me too," I said.

The vibration of my phone made me jump.

"I'll go now," said Zeta, making a clumsy exit before I had a chance to say anything else.

I picked up my phone and saw I had a text message from a number that wasn't saved to my contacts.

Hi Kate. It's Monro. On a pay as you go. What news about Clemmie?

Monro! My thumbs manically tapped back a message about nobody knowing what really happened yet.

I waited, my thumbs poised over the keyboard:

You think she fell or was pushed? came back the reply.

I don't know. It's horrible whatever. So are you where I thought you were?

??

Did you get my text?

No. We ditched our phones. Where do you think we are?

I typed the S of Scotland, and then stopped. I had an uncomfortable feeling. What if it wasn't Monro? What if someone was hoping I'd give his location away? I deleted the S and typed:

Tell me the name of the boat at Thornley harbour first.

I don't understand?

He wouldn't have forgotten *Tiger Lily*. This didn't feel right. I turned off my phone and placed it under my pillow, curling up next to it. I felt cold, as if it had turned autumnal in the last ten minutes. I pictured my parents in the relentless sunshine of Dubai, and not for the first time wondered how much – or how little – they thought about me when I wasn't there.

I could hear Meribel on her phone through the wall. Her voice was loud and animated, as if the reception at the other end wasn't very good. Within seconds of the call ending she was at my door, and I sat up.

"Hey, Kate!" she said. "The modelling job in Japan's got the go-ahead. Six days and loads of money. And, oh my God, isn't it lucky I love sushi?"

She bounced on to my bed, and I knew my voice lacked the required enthusiasm as I said, "When do you go?"

"The day after tomorrow. And if anyone here says I can't go, that's tough because I'm going anyway. The only people who can stop me are the police, and I've told them everything I know, which is diddly squat."

"That's so soon," I mumbled, because I was mostly saying it in my head.

"To tell the truth, I'm happy about that. The vibe is terrible round here." Meribel got off the bed and went into my bathroom to gaze at herself in the mirror. "This thing right here better not be a super-sized spot brewing," she muttered and came back out, rubbing her cheek.

"I don't want you to go," I said.

Meribel stared at me. "Talk to Lo."

"She doesn't want to talk to me."

I understood the way she nodded after I said this. She knew how bad this was, that Lo might never speak to me again.

"There's a printout of me on Veronica's artwork with the word 'fake' on it. Did you know?"

"Nope." I saw she was surprised. "That's mean. Nothing to do with me. Lo wouldn't have done that either. Paige?"

"How many people have you told?"

Anger flared in her cheeks. "Listen, Kate. Lo and I haven't told anyone apart from Sneller, even though we don't owe you anything. Maybe someone heard me and Lo talking. You know what this place is like. Stop feeling so sorry for yourself and face what you did. Deal with it." She left my room and slammed the door.

CHAPTER 25

At dinner, I sat with Zeta, but at the same table as Meribel and Lo, so not everyone would work out Lo wasn't talking to me. Calding wasn't at dinner, and the fourth-formers at our table – the only ones who were chatting – said Calding was bound to either quit because of the stress or be sacked any day now. I skipped dessert, murmuring to Zeta I was going to Davison's common room. She asked if I wanted her to come too, but I said no. I regretted saying it so forcefully, but I didn't want anyone with me.

I'd timed it right and the common room was empty. It had the air of being abandoned. Clemmie would never be in here again, and who knew when Monro and Veronica would be back.

217

The printout on Veronica's artwork was from my Instagram account, the only photo of my face I'd ever posted. It was taken a summer ago, a head and shoulders shot, with a bright blue Mediterranean sky as the background. I was wearing a white top and I looked symmetrical and happy. On the printout, someone had written FAKE in thick black pen across my forehead and stuck it in the centre of the artwork. What Zeta hadn't told me was the person had also drawn arrows pointing to my ears, eye and nose and chin. I took it down and folded it, and the crease went right across my mouth. There was so much pinned up there now. The photo of the Amber Park Hospital was underneath printouts that didn't make any sense to me, but maybe made someone else uncomfortable, such as a picture of a South-East London council estate, and an article about a protest outside a factory in Wales. A lot of things were taken down by the people they were aimed at, but you didn't want to be seen with anything incriminating, or it would be taken as confirmation that an accusation might be true or a raw nerve had been hit.

The door opened, and in came Paige with a couple of her group. They looked diminished without Clemmie, uncertain which level of bitchiness to use. Paige walked up to the artwork, and the other two went to play pool giving me amused glances at the folded sheet of paper in my hand as they did.

"You've been allowed back, then?" Paige said. "I heard you used to be super-ugly, and your dad remodelled you."

I made a great effort not to show any emotion. "I heard there was a day last decade when you were a nice person."

Paige rolled her eyes and said, "You need to work on your comebacks." She leaned against a table. "What d'you know about Veronica and Monro?"

I thought about the strange text messages. "Nothing," I said. "What do you know?"

"Must be embarrassing for you thinking you were tight with Monro, and you don't know anything about where he is or why he and Vee ran away together. What's it like to fancy a murder suspect?"

I gave her my finest pitying look. I wanted to leave but not if there was a danger she thought she'd driven me away, so I went through the motions of putting the kettle on to make myself a cup of tea.

Paige said, "I'll tell you what I know: Veronica Steppleton is the main suspect in the case."

"What?"

There was a tiny wobble in her voice. "I heard Clemmie arguing with Veronica when I was with Rob."

"Are you *sure* it was Veronica?" I wondered if Paige regretted that she'd stayed with Rob when she heard the argument.

She said, "One hundred per cent, and it was a bad argument."

I imagined a confrontation between Clemmie and Veronica, Veronica jabbing Clemmie's chest to drive a point home, Clemmie stumbling. Could it have happened like that? Would Veronica and Monro have run?

Veronica had a suitcase. Her running away appeared planned. Was the argument with Clemmie also planned?

Whatever had happened, it didn't look good for her.

I held up the folded piece of paper in my hand while Paige was being relatively open. "Did you do this?"

Paige smirked. "I wish I had."

The other two girls were whispering to each other by the pool table. I stepped closer to Paige and said quietly, "How did Clemmie know about my surgery?"

"She was in touch with people who knew people," said Paige vaguely.

So she didn't know. It must have upset her that Clemmie hadn't trusted her.

Paige's face hardened. "There's something I want to say to you, Kate: Miss Sneller is asking for people to speak or contribute to Clemmie's concert on Saturday. If you volunteer, I'll make sure you regret it."

I stopped myself saying that I wouldn't ever have considered speaking at the memorial. I wasn't a complete hypocrite.

"Clemmie loathed you," said Paige. "You swept in to the third form all pleased with yourself and the way you look and thought you knew everything. But you didn't. You fake." She looked me up and down with disdain, and went to join the other two.

I took a deep breath and steadied myself. I was going to

unpin everything off Veronica's artwork. This had gone far enough.

As I piled up the papers, pressing them flat, reducing them to a bundle of a few millimetres thick, it occurred to me I might be tampering with evidence. I wouldn't throw it all out. I'd hand it to Miss Sneller when I was sent to see her.

It was lonely going to bed without saying goodnight to Bel and Lo. I listened to a podcast about sculpture techniques which was boring enough to send me to sleep. I was jolted awake by my phone ringing. My immediate thought was Elsie Gran.

My phone screen showed it wasn't her. It was Monro. He was calling from his actual phone.

"Kate?" His voice was both familiar and distant.

I sat up immediately. "Yes, it's me. Did you message me earlier today on another phone?"

"No. Why?"

"Someone pretending to be you was trying to find out where you were. What's going on?"

"I don't know," he said. He was talking fast and too softly. "We read in a newspaper yesterday that Vee's the main suspect in Clemmie's death. We didn't even know anything had happened to Clemmie until a few days ago. And now I think something's happened to Vee. She went out to get some food and hasn't come back."

"Slow down," I said. "Where are you?"

"A village on the east coast of Scotland. In a holiday cottage that belongs to friends of Vee's parents. They don't know we're here, but Vee knew where the key was hidden. I switched off my phone for days but now I don't care any more. I think the police have got Vee." His voice cracked. He sounded exhausted.

"Why did you and Veronica take off like you did?"

"I'll explain everything soon," said Monro. "There's something you need to know about me. It's a hard thing to tell someone. And now I think it's too late."

I heard shouting in the background.

"That's the police," said Monro. "I'm freaking out."

"It'll be OK," I said.

"Please will you do something?" Monro asked in an urgent voice. He didn't stop to hear my answer. "Vee was muttering before she left about a delivery note that's pinned on her artwork. She said she hoped it didn't get taken down before she had a chance to check it out. When I asked what she was talking about, she said it was for those sweat pads and it was probably nothing. If Vee's a suspect, I have to do everything I can to help her."

"Sure," I said.

I heard louder shouting.

"I think they might bash the door down," said Monro.

"Open the door," I said. "Don't make it worse."

"Can you keep it safe?" asked Monro, talking even faster.

"Yes, let me find it now. I took everything off her artwork to give to Miss Sneller." I switched on my bedside

222

light, climbed out of bed and started going through the pile of paper, my phone clamped under my chin, worried that somehow I hadn't collected everything, or it was missing. I recoiled as I saw the printout of me with *Fake* across my forehead.

"Hide it somewhere when you find it," said Monro.

I kept leafing through the pile, and then it was there in front of me – the delivery note for three boxes of ten stick-on underarm sweat pads from an online pharmacy which had appeared around the time of the dress receipts for the Pankhurst party. The top had been cut off for anonymity, probably by Veronica, so I couldn't see who had ordered them, or any order number.

"I've got it," I said. "But I don't see how—"

"That's good. Don't keep it in your room. It might really matter," said Monro. I thought it would calm him down to know I had it in my hands, but he seemed to be even more agitated than before. "Be careful who you trust. Look, I have to go. I don't want to be shot by the police. That was a joke. Kind of." He was trying not to cry.

"The police aren't going to accuse Veronica or you of doing anything you haven't done," I said desperately. "Just tell them everything you know." I didn't want to end the conversation.

"Take care, Kate. Please," he said.

"You too," I whispered. He had to be the one to end this call.

"Bye, then, Kate." I could tell he didn't want to hang up either. There was so much unsaid in his voice.

Then the phone went dead, and I deleted my recent call history.

I held the delivery note, smaller than A4 because the details at the top had been cut off. The contact details for an online pharmacy were along the bottom of it.

I reached for my laptop and looked it up. It was UK based and it specialized in natural products and embarrassing problems.

I chewed the side of my thumbnail. What was its significance?

All my instincts told me Monro had nothing to do with Clemmie's death, but Veronica... I didn't think so, but I wasn't sure. I'd hide the delivery note for now. I could always hand it in at a later point. Where was a good place to hide it, though? Somewhere close by that wouldn't be disturbed. It took me several minutes to think through all Pankhurst's communal places, where no one would ever imagine something would be hidden. The painting of the boarding house founder in the dining hall – that was perfect. I'd attach the paper to the back of it with Blu-Tack, and the weight of the painting itself would help keep it in place.

It was against the rules to be out of my bedroom, so I'd need an extremely good excuse. I folded the receipt in two and stuffed it along with a blob of Blu-Tack and my keys from home in the pocket of my dressing gown, and then crept on to the third-floor landing. Soft built-in nightlights at skirting-board level lit the stairs and hallways. The old building was never silent at night, shifting and creaking.

I felt uneasy as I trod carefully past Clemmie's bedroom.

The dining room smelled stale, as if there was still leftover food somewhere. Side lamps in the hall which switched on at night emitted enough light for me to make my way to the founder's painting, lift the bottom edge and press the receipt on to the back. I prayed the whole painting was secure on its wire and wouldn't come crashing down. It seemed to be, although it juddered alarmingly when I straightened it.

I ran to the stairs, exhaling heavily from having held my breath so long in the dining hall, and took them two at time. Two thirds of the way up the second staircase my heart double-thudded. At the top was Ms Calding. She was in a white towelling dressing gown, grey stripy pyjamas visible underneath, and old person slippers. Her hair was down and she looked different, like a Pankhurst student.

"What are you doing, Miss Jordan-Ferreira?" If I'd given her a shock by being out of my room, she didn't show it.

I pulled out my key ring, showing her the little fluffy bird toy attached. It had been the best I could do. "I left this in my coat pocket downstairs," I said. "My gran gave it to me. I couldn't sleep without it." Fortunately she didn't know Elsie Gran well enough to know she'd have never given me anything so cutesy. It had come from Lo.

Calding didn't react with any sympathy. "I'm giving you five behaviour points. Don't let me find you outside your room at night again. Understood?"

I nodded. It was around two-thirty in the morning. It wasn't normal for her to be walking around. "Now go to bed." She stood and watched as I made my way along the landing to the third staircase. As I walked past Clemmie's room I noticed that the door was slightly ajar. I was fairly certain it had been closed when I had gone downstairs.

CHAPTER 26

At breakfast everyone was buzzing with the news that Monro and Veronica had been found in a remote farm cottage. Most of the sixth-formers from Davison had come over to see what the latest was. I couldn't help glancing up at the founder's painting as I pretended to eat my honey-nut cornflakes. There was no hint of white paper visible at the back of it, thank goodness.

I'd sat with Meribel and Lo, for the sake of appearances, but I knew they'd rather I wasn't there. We were near a clump of noisy first-formers who didn't even know Veronica and Monro, but who were speculating wildly about them. I pictured Monro and Veronica being interviewed separately. What bound

227

them together so deeply? Was it really just about being childhood friends?

Meribel said she had to get up at five-thirty the next morning for her trip to Japan and she hadn't even told Sneller yet. I thought of my own inevitable interview with the head now she was aware of my part in Sasha's expulsion. Much as I dreaded it, it would be a relief. I decided I would go to speak to her this morning rather than wait to be summoned.

Squirrel brought me a hot chocolate, which she always did when she saw someone wasn't eating. The Ghost and Calding spoke together in a corner, and then Calding clapped her hands and asked for quiet.

"Would fifth- and sixth-formers stay behind, please?" When everybody else had left, she made us bunch together around one long table, and told us some papers had been removed from Veronica's artwork and as they might or might not be evidence in Clemmie's case, she needed them handed in.

Paige's face looked gleeful. "Kate took them yesterday. I'm a witness."

I nodded and sat up straight. "Yes, I did. There was some toxic stuff there," I said. I was Kate Lynette Jordan-Ferreira. I was House Prefect and fearless.

A sixth-former echoed the word toxic and sniggered. I glared at her, and she stopped.

"You didn't bin them, though, did you?" said Paige accusingly. "You took them away."

"I was going to hand them in to Miss Sneller." I stood up. "I'll go and get them."

Calding nodded at the Ghost. "It's OK, Kate. Mrs Haven will go up to your room now. Where are they?"

I nodded. "On my chest of drawers." Were they really looking for that delivery note?

Calding kept us a few minutes more, talking about arrangements for Clemmie's concert.

After we were dismissed and went to leave the dining hall, Calding caught my eye and said, "I trust you got to sleep in the end, Miss Jordan-Ferreira?" and I said, "Yes, thank you."

"What was that about?" asked Meribel, climbing next to me on the staircase. I was aware of Lo keeping her distance a few steps behind us.

"No idea," I said.

"Why did she ask if you'd got to sleep in the end?"

I opened my mouth to tell her, but said, "She must have heard me moving about in my room on one of her patrols," because I remembered Monro's words. *Be careful who you trust.*

When Meribel went into her room, I waited for Lo and said, "Please can I talk with you?"

"There's nothing left to say," said Lo. She went to close her door, but I placed my foot in the way. "Please? Two minutes?"

Lo let go of the door, and carried on into her room as if she didn't care one way or the other. I followed her as she went to the bathroom and picked up her toothbrush.

"I'm going to see Miss Sneller this morning," I said.

"Good," said Lo, as she squeezed toothpaste on her toothbrush.

"I regret what I did so badly. I'm sorry, Lo. For everything."

"Forget it," said Lo. "It's way too late to apologize." She brushed her upper teeth on one side.

"I wasn't the only person who was scared to stand up to Clemmie. Zeta told me—"

Lo spat out toothpaste into the basin. "Don't make this about anybody else. You let someone else take the blame for something you knew they hadn't done. You let an innocent person be *expelled*." She gave me a look of hatred. "Because you're off-the-scale vain. If Sneller expels you, you'll just end up in some other fancy school. For Sasha, being at this school meant everything to her and her family. Now get out of my room." She turned on the tap and swooshed away the toothpaste spit to mark the end of the conversation.

After registration, I went to Miss Snellers's office and told her assistant that I would sit and wait to be seen. I was informed there was a scheduled meeting, and I should go back to class and wait to be called. But I insisted on staying, and the assistant eventually gave up and waved half-heartedly towards the stiff-backed, orange-felt sofa.

When I was eventually shown into Miss Sneller's office, she looked pained to see me, as if I was causing an immense amount of work for her. She put on her glasses and said, "If you're here about your failure to disclose all the facts when asked about Sasha Mires and Clementine Hillard, please go ahead." She picked up a silver pen and held it expectantly above a pile of loose blank paper.

I told her how I'd lied, and allowed Clemmie to blackmail me, and she scribbled away. It seemed at times the sound of her pen on the paper was as loud as my voice. After a bit, she muttered about emerging details, and how there was a lot to unravel. I said nothing as she told me it appeared I'd fallen short of Mount Norton's *extremely high standards.*

Did she genuinely believe Mount Norton had extremely high standards?

"I'm in the process of considering how we move forward with this development," she said. "Of course, you'll have to speak to the police again." She sighed. "It's delicate ... with Clemmie's family ... and I believe Lois said she'd heard Sasha was very ill at present."

"Was Clemmie applying for the Longton scholarship too?" I asked.

Miss Sneller frowned. "After that paper was found, the scholarship wasn't awarded this academic year." She'd avoided my question. She asked what I knew about the man we called Kipper. Had he ever approached me to do anything?

"Like what?" I asked.

"There have been reports of him attempting to recruit Mount Norton students to sell drugs," she said, and placed her pen down.

Was that what Kipper had meant by asking if we were interested in part-time work? Was that something else Clemmie had started to do to bring in cash while pretending she was loaded?

"While the investigation continues, the concert will be a chance for everyone to come together and reflect, a chance for Mount Norton to show that although we make mistakes we learn from them and..." She rambled on in her assembly voice. Eventually, she picked up the pile of paper and tapped the end of it on the desk to make a *rap-rap-rap* sound, and looked at her watch. "Was that all for now?"

"There's something else," I said.

"Oh?"

"It's about Bernard. He..." I couldn't find the right words.

Miss Sneller interlaced her hands. It felt too formal. "Fire away," she said. "Give me your side of the story."

"My side?"

"Bernard came to see me yesterday. It's OK. I'm not here to judge." She gave an impatient nod, indicating I should hurry up.

I needed to consider my words like the pebbles at Thornley harbour, the weight and colour of each one. "We kissed once, last term, but afterwards I made it clear—"

Miss Sneller sighed and interrupted. "May I suggest you keep well away from each other? If your obsessive thoughts continue, please book yourself an appointment with the school counsellor. We will do our best to support you."

Obsessive thoughts? Had Bernard said I was obsessed with him?

Miss Sneller took off her glasses and gazed out of her window. She had one of the best views of the sea. That morning it was choppy and cold-looking. "You know, this school has a lot to deal with right now and I want you to remember your role in it." She gazed at me. "Is that all, Miss Jordan-Ferreira?"

I nodded, my mouth dry. I understood I was being dismissed in more ways than one. I stood up. Miss Sneller was rubbing her eye as if she was tired. She wanted everything swept away. She cared about Mount Norton as an institution more than she cared about any person there.

I didn't bother going to English. It was one of the other subjects I had with Bernard. I sat on a bench outside the performing arts block, my knees up against my chest, and watched the sea. I thought about Monro and Veronica being questioned somewhere.

At lunchtime I picked up a sandwich and went to the art room to work on my hands sculpture. Mr Hayes was talking to a technician and he jumped when he saw me. There was a panicked expression on his face.

"It's OK if I work on my sculpture, isn't it?" I said, walking towards the cupboard.

He reached the door before me. "No. I mean ordinarily yes, but I've..." His shoulders slumped and he looked stricken. "A little earlier I made the most appalling discovery. Your sculpture must have fallen off the shelf. I was going to contact you but I wanted to speak to you in person. I knew how upset you'd be..." He trailed off. He opened the door. "I'm most terribly sorry."

"I can mend it though." I turned it into a question. "It's not fired yet."

Mr Hayes said, "I'm afraid it's completely smashed."

With a clogged throat, I watched him switch the light on in the cupboard and I scanned the shelves for the round wooden board I'd placed it on. The paper clay was no longer covered in plastic. About fifty or sixty – maybe more – pieces lay on the board. Greyish lumps of dried-out clay. I swallowed a sob and reached for one that looked like a fingertip. Separated from the rest of its hand, it looked grotesque. I couldn't help thinking of Clemmie's body, smashed on the rocks, broken beyond repair. My gut rolled inside me like a churning sea and I took a deep breath.

"I put the board in the corner," I said. "How could it have fallen?"

Mr Hayes pointed to a patch of floor. "I found it here. Perhaps someone caught it with their clothing. It's very bad form not to have said anything. I'll be speaking to all the art classes about this." He stood watching me nervously while I decided my sculpture hadn't landed on the floor accidentally. Bernard had done this.

"I'll make some more paper clay for you," said Mr Hayes. "I'll have it ready for your next lesson."

I nodded and mumbled my thanks. The cupboard was too warm and if I stayed any longer I'd be sick. I left the art room and went outside to lean against the building and breathe in fresh air. I looked at a poster in the window next to me. *Concert for Clemmie.* The nausea swelled. I reached into my bag for my phone. I didn't want to be here any more. Elsie Gran wouldn't need to be asked twice to come and pick me up.

Her phone rang and rang. There was a click as it was answered and I waited for Elsie Gran to say hello, but instead I heard, "This is Maria. Nothing to worry about, love. Your gran's got flu and I'm over here making sure she's getting enough fluids. What's that, Elsie?" There was a pause. "Your gran says she hopes you're OK and haven't caught it. You're OK, love, aren't you?" Maria didn't even wait for my response before I heard her say to Elsie Gran, "Kate says she's fine, Elsie. She was just phoning for a chat. You were phoning for a chat, weren't you?"

It takes me a moment, but I say, "Yes, I was only checking in." I sent my love and said I'd phone again tomorrow, and I thanked Maria for looking after her.

"That's what friends are for," she said, and that's what made me cry after I'd ended the call.

I walked out of the school grounds without permission and went back to Pankhurst, telling the Ghost, who was in the office, that I had a migraine and had to lie down or I'd vomit. She told me to leave my bedroom door open and insisted on checking me once every half hour. I asked where Calding was, and she said solemnly, "She had to take the afternoon off for personal reasons," and wouldn't tell me anything else.

I must have fallen asleep because when I woke the light had faded and I could hear the noise downstairs of girls coming in after the school day. I lay on my bed, pretending to be asleep when the dinner bell rang. The Furball came in with food on a tray, saying she'd been drafted in at short notice and if I was still ill tomorrow morning I'd have to go to the sick bay in the main school. If Wibbz was still here, I'd have been allowed at least a couple of days in bed before being carted away to the main school. I closed my eyes.

"It's very busy without Ms Calding here," said the Furball. "I have to go back downstairs."

I didn't respond.

I woke up in the night, still fully dressed, and ate cold Squirrel stew. Then I dozed until I was jolted awake by Meribel crashing around her room. It was five-thirty. Of course: she was leaving for Japan. I got up and went into her room. Lo was helping Meribel close an overpacked case on the bed. They both looked at me awkwardly.

"I thought you were ill," said Meribel.

Lo looked away and went back to edging the zipper round the suitcase.

"Have a good time," I said. It came out flat and wrong.

Meribel nodded. It was the moment when we should have hugged, but she checked the time on her phone and said, "I've got five minutes until my taxi's here."

"I'll leave you to it," I said, and left her room. I sat up against the headboard on my bed, listening to the thump of the suitcase hitting the floor, and Bel and Lo murmuring to each other, and then the rapid thumps of the case being dragged down the stairs.

I sent a text to Maria saying if Elsie Gran became worse she had to let me know, and then I got up and put my dressing gown on over my school clothes, pushed my feet into sliders, and went to sit outside on the fire escape. I could hear the slam of a car door – the taxi probably – from the other side of the building, followed by the sound of it driving away. Perhaps I couldn't sleep because I'd slept so much the previous afternoon. I sat on the cold metal, leaned my head against the railings, and watched the sky change from grey to gold to various shades of blue. I had no idea what time it was, but I could hear an early morning delivery van pull up and Squirrel complain loudly about something.

A low whistle came from Churchill, then another. I stood. I so wanted it to be Monro that I almost didn't look because I couldn't bear the disappointment if it wasn't, but I did.

It was him, and I didn't hesitate. I clambered down the fire escape in my clothes, sliders and dressing gown to meet him.

CHAPTER 27

He reached out to me as soon as I was in touching distance, and pulled me towards him. When our lips met, I could have sworn they fizzed, and we kissed as if we might be pulled apart any moment.

"Are they expelling you?" I asked when we eventually stopped.

"I don't know," he said. "I'm waiting to find out."

I supposed I was in the same uncertain situation, depending on what Miss Sneller decided.

Monro took my hand and appraised my outfit with a smile, but didn't comment. We walked to the bench and huddled as close together as we could without damaging our internal organs. He touched my calf and I said, "I'd keep away from my feet if I were you. They probably stink. I slept in these tights."

He pretended to reel backwards but kept hold of my leg. I laughed at his reaction while wishing I hadn't spent twenty-four hours in the same clothes.

"I wasn't feeling good, but I'm fine now," I said, then added, "Apart from needing a shower."

He shook his head as if he couldn't keep up with what I was talking about, but his smile told me he didn't care what clothes I was wearing.

"Is Veronica back too?" I asked.

His face became serious again. "She went back to her parents' house. The police took our phones, and when I tried to call her on her home landline, nobody picked up. I don't think she's allowed to speak to me. The police are trying to pin Clemmie's fall on Vee. There's a witness saying they had an argument. It's serious. They say even if Vee didn't push Clemmie, she threatened her and caused the fall. Manslaughter."

"Paige is the witness," I said. "But . . . weren't you with her? You were a witness too."

"I'd gone on ahead," said Monro. "I was putting her suitcase in the car. She said she wanted to speak to Clemmie on her own. Veronica said Clemmie shouldn't be hanging out with Kipper. She'd heard things about him, not just getting kids into dealing, but being properly stalkerish."

I nodded.

"They argued. Clemmie didn't want to hear what she had to say. Vee's tried hard to be good to Clemmie even though there was bad feeling between their parents over money. It wasn't Vee's fault. Any of it."

"Did you see Bernard? Or Kipper?"

Monro shook his head. "That doesn't mean they weren't hiding there, though." He shuddered.

I put an arm round him. "What's the sweat pad receipt about? I swear Calding and the Ghost are looking for it."

"I wish I knew," said Monro. "The police took me and Vee to separate police stations." He paused and from the way he was breathed in, I guessed he was trying to get a grip of his emotions. "See if you can get in touch with Vee. I'll never be able to reach her. I'm not her parents' favourite person right now. If it wasn't for me, we wouldn't have run away."

"So why..." I took my arm away and spoke slowly because I really wanted the answer to the question but feared it at the same time. "Why did you and Veronica run away together?"

I felt Monro tense. He removed his hand from my leg and sat up straighter. "There's no easy way to tell you this."

"Spit it out. You're making this weird."

He looked at the ground. "I have a thing which Vee knows about. It's degenerative." He looked up at me.

"Are you deliberately trying to confuse me?"

"I have a disease which affects my muscles, and it might

240

get worse. It might improve slightly, but not completely. Or it might stay the same. No one knows for sure."

"Oh," I said. I did my best not to sound shocked. "That sucks."

He nodded. "Yep, it really does. In the summer I was told I might get to a point where I wouldn't be allowed to drive a regular car any more. I'd need an adapted one."

I remembered times when he'd been unsteady. He'd broken his ankle at the beach café party last year. Veronica's concern about him standing on the stool in the beach house, his neoprene leg braces at running club.

"It's a rare disease with a ridiculous name," he said, "and there's no regular pattern to it. Vee said we should just take off. Screw school. Have a driving adventure. That was what her art project was about. My hidden disease. She asked if I minded. By the time I did mind, it was too late. At least the money paid for our petrol and other things on our trip. She's giving the rest to a research charity."

The things we keep hidden.

I could hear Veronica suggest a driving adventure. I could see her campaigning on Monro's behalf for the charity. And I could understand his reluctance for it to become public.

"I love my grandad's car. I can't get insurance on it at the moment until we know more about my condition, so I shouldn't be driving. My parents thought it was locked away in my uncle's garage. The whole thing makes me so angry. It used to make me nuts, proper nuts, so I guess it's better now." His jaw clenched. "But I don't think I'll ever not be angry about it."

I felt angry for him too.

He couldn't look me in the eye any more. "I wish I hadn't told you."

"Why?" I slipped my arm under his and leaned my head against his shoulder, so he wasn't confronted by my confusion.

"Everything will change between us. You'll feel sorry for me, like Vee does."

I lifted my head. "You want a pity kiss?" Our lips pressed against each other with a new pressure, tender but still urgent.

"Pity kisses aren't so bad," he said. As his hands moved inside my dressing gown, the bell sounded loudly in Churchill.

We reluctantly pulled away from each other, getting up from the bench, and Monro said, "I need to go. I'm on a final-final warning. Walk with me to the entrance."

I walked as far as I dared, and took off my dressing gown so I was just in school uniform and less conspicuous, but I was still a girl in the grounds of a boys' boarding house. We kissed goodbye, and I turned and made my way back to the gate.

I showered, changed into clean uniform and, as soon as it was eight o'clock, I phoned up customer services at the online pharmacy. The female voice which answered on the third ring was efficient and cheerful.

"If I give you an address and the item ordered, please can you tell me the name of the person who ordered it?" I asked.

"I'm sorry, what?"

I repeated it, glad the person at the other end couldn't see my face. It sounded bizarre to me too.

"What's the order number?" The cheeriness in her voice had been replaced with impatience.

"I don't have that," I said. "Can you just look up the address and see who ordered three packs of sweat pads?"

"I'm sorry," said the lady, in a voice I imagined was reserved for not very bright customers. "I'm not allowed to access that information for you, I'm afraid. Anything else I can help you with today?"

"Er ... no thanks. Thanks anyway." I hung up and cringed.

School was manageable because I knew Monro was there. The morning dragged, but at last it was lunch. We sat at the end of a long table in the main dining hall, and I blocked out the sound of everyone else. I told him about my phone call to the website, and he said, "Maybe Veronica meant some other bit of paper?" He pulled apart a bread roll. "Was there anything else on that noticeboard to do with sweating?"

I shook my head.

Monro eased a post-it note out of his trouser pocket

and gave it to me. "Here. I've written out Vee's parents' landline for you. See if you can speak to her." He dipped some of his roll into the tomato and basil soup in front of him and said, "Bring me up to speed on what I've missed."

I took a deep breath and began with my surgeries. I had to.

He studied my face as I knew he would. To cover up my awkwardness, I kept talking. I told him how I'd watched Sasha be expelled and kept quiet. He looked shocked but didn't comment. I couldn't stop talking – I described the visit to the hospital and my fallout with Lo, the printout which outed me as a fake, and about Bernard. I looked at my hands as I described what had happened at the beach house and he swore in a low voice, pushing away his bowl so hard the soup slopped over the edge.

"I want to. . . You don't want to hear what I want to do to him," he said, and put his hand on my arm. "I'm sorry I wasn't there, Kate. I should have been there for you."

I rubbed the smooth edge of my thumbnail with my forefinger.

"Have you reported him?"

"Yes." I made painful eye contact with him. "It's his word against mine."

Monro screwed his face up as if he couldn't believe it. "I saw him push a girl hard against a wall in the first form," he said. "We got in a fight about it. He came off worse. Next time, you won't recognize him."

I placed my hand in his. "Leave it. Let's talk about something else," I said.

"This isn't over," said Monro.

"I know," I said. Some things were never over.

After school, I walked back with Monro. We took our time, going the extra-long way by the sea, holding hands and stopping to kiss in the bus shelter. When other people showed up, we moved on.

I wasn't hungry for any after-school snacks, and neither was he. The most obvious way to be together at this time of day was to go to Davison. I hoped there wouldn't be many people in there, but I could tell from the noise as we walked up the corridor there was a crowd.

Monro was at the door before me. He could see something through the glass square that shocked him. "Oh no," he breathed.

I pushed open the door, and saw everybody was standing round Veronica's collage. I could see the edge of some black spray-paint writing. There was a capital C and then an O. I pushed my way forward, and as people let me through, I saw the whole word: *COWARD*.

Was it meant for me?

CHAPTER 28

Word must have got back to Pankhurst via someone because the Ghost was suddenly at the door, and Calding too, who I hadn't realized was back. She looked ill. Her cheeks were blotchy and sunken, and her eyes smaller, as if the skin around them had swollen. The two of them didn't break their strides – they came in and between them lifted the artwork off the wall.

"Dreadful," said the Ghost. They eyed it when they had it on the floor. The Ghost touched the large black letters and then checked her fingers. The paint had come off on to them slightly.

"Show's over," said Calding to us. "I'll be having a meeting with the Davison staff about this. I want

246

statements from everyone here on my desk by tomorrow morning telling me everything you know about this artwork and graffiti. OK?"

When we didn't answer sufficiently loudly, she repeated herself. Monro raised his eyebrows at me but I squeezed the side of my mouth in reply. Churchill boys hadn't witnessed enough of Calding to know her brusque manner.

We sat around quietly after the Ghost and Calding had left. Everyone seemed to think the graffiti was aimed at Veronica because she hadn't come back to school. Paige said whoever had done it was spot on, and Monro told her to piss off.

They shouted at each other until I stood between them and screamed for them to stop. Paige stormed out, followed by a few of her crew, and Monro sat at a table, propping up his head with his hands. As I made him a cup of tea, I thought of my trashed sculpture, and noted Bernard was conveniently absent.

Hugo said loudly he'd have got rid of the artwork far earlier if he'd been in charge.

I muttered, "Of course you would."

As the room got back to its normal level of conversation, Flo quizzed Monro about why he and Veronica had run away, and everyone trailed off talking, waiting for his answer. He rubbed his forehead, and looked at me.

I nodded slightly. *Tell the truth.*

He told them some of it. Said Veronica knew he was unhappy, and they'd planned to do a road trip, but it had nothing to do with Clemmie's death. They hadn't known about Clemmie until they'd seen a newspaper a couple of days ago.

"I regret taking off like that," he said. "But I can't change the past, so." He looked at me as he said it.

We were asked to wear bright colours to Clemmie's concert. It made me think of Veronica, not Clemmie, who'd always worn more understated colours. In between pieces performed by the choir, orchestra and solo performers, one of Clemmie's crew recited a poem – which was odd because Clemmie couldn't stand poetry. Paige read out a speech saying what a fine person Clemmie had been, and Miss Sneller talked about what a great loss she was to the vibrant school community.

I thought of the awful way Clemmie had died and hoped it had been quick.

Staff sat on chairs round the edge of the assembly hall as usual, to keep an eye on students. Several of them were red-eyed and clutching tissues. The Ghost's beige-with-make-up face was flushed, but she sat with a straight back. In contrast, Calding next to her was hunched over. She didn't glance round at us once, and it was up to the Ghost and our form tutors to frown at anybody who was whispering. Clemmie's parents sat at the front. They were with the senior staff, a few adults I didn't recognize, and Wibbz.

All of us at Pankhurst who'd known Wibbz strained to see her. We couldn't see her face, but her puffy brown hair was exactly the same. Her head wobbled from side to side during the musical parts. At the end of the concert there was some ceremonial candle lighting and a prayer, and we processed out of the assembly hall in silence for tea and cake in the dining hall.

Conversations erupted as soon as there was some distance from the assembly hall, and we were funnelled into the main dining hall, past tables of cups and saucers, and plates of piled up cake. Squirrel was behind a table in a green dress pouring tea out of a large teapot: I don't think I'd ever seen her out of her Pankhurst kitchen uniform. Clemmie's bewildered parents were being escorted by two sixth-formers who had probably never snuck out to the beach at night and had certainly never been to any boarding-house parties. They were the sort of students Clemmie would have mocked behind their backs.

"I hate this," said Zeta, suddenly by my side. Her teacup rattled in its saucer as she held it. "I want to go back to Pankhurst."

"You don't need to stay long," I said. "Let's say hello to Wibbz."

She was easy to spot. There was a crowd of Pankhurst girls around her. She was squeezing cheeks and exclaiming loudly at everyone. When she saw me, she said, "Here's the beautiful Kate Jordan-Ferreira!" and took my hand. "How are you doing? How's the top floor? Do you miss me?"

I smelled alcohol on her breath. "I'm OK, thanks," I said.

"Fantastic!" she said. "You girls must tell me everything. I've missed you."

She didn't seem like the amusing Wibbz character I remembered. She seemed desperate, hanging on to girls' arms and leaning in too close. Her laughter seemed false, her questions veering towards intrusive. *Has your mum remarried? Did I hear your dad's warehouse caught on fire? How do you like the new housemistress? What did your brother get in his exams?*

She took a sip of tea from her cup, and said in a loud voice, "I must say I'd rather have something stronger at such a sad event. What a terrible thing to happen to a lovely, lovely girl."

The Ghost, who was circulating with a plate of mini Victoria sponges, thrust the plate towards Wibbz, who took one, nodded her thanks, and said, "Clementine was one of my favourites."

The Ghost gave a professional smile, and said, "All Pankhurst girls are your favourites, aren't they, Miss Wibberton?"

"Oh yes," said Wibbz. She stopped to take a bite of the cake. Cream oozed out on to her mouth. She wiped it with the back of her hand, and licked it. Instead of catching someone's eye and smiling, I felt repulsed. "I loved every single girl," said Wibbz. "Clemmie was a real pal, though." She took another bite of the cake and cream dripped on to her silky blouse. While she searched for a tissue in her handbag, I slipped away to find Monro. I'd go back to rescue Zeta if she needed it later.

I reached Monro at the same time as Miss Sneller's assistant. I was close enough to hear her say, "Monro, the police would like you to answer a few more questions. If you walk back to Churchill, I'll phone ahead for one of your house parents to give you a lift to the police station."

"Oh great. More questions," said Monro, his shoulders slumping. "When is this going to end?"

"I'll walk back with you," I said, standing next to him, and tucked my hand in his.

It was a relief to be outside, away from the pretence that Clemmie was the greatest Mount Nortonian to walk England's green and pleasant land. I would have savoured this time with Monro down the empty drive on any other day. The huge lawns either side had been freshly mown, and at the gates, the huge terracotta flower tubs had been replanted for today with sombre purple plants and bluey-green foliage.

"What d'you think the police need from me?" asked Monro. "I've told them everything I know."

I shrugged. "Don't panic, it's probably just paperwork. Routine double-checking stuff."

Monro shook his head and looked up at the sky. "When I left the station before, they said I was free go home or come back to school. My parents gave me the choice." He squeezed my hand. "I chose you."

Everything swelled inside me. This was almost what it felt like to be insanely happy, except I couldn't be because I'd just been to a memorial concert for a dead fifteen-year-old, and because Monro wasn't happy either. He was frightened.

"The police do that," I said. "They check, then they check again, to see if they've missed anything." I had no idea about police procedures but saying that seemed to calm him a bit.

At Churchill's front door, we kissed, and I burrowed my head into Monro's neck, inhaling the scent of his warm, clean skin.

The front door was then opened by a housemaster who said, "No dawdling outside, lad."

"Is that what you call it, sir?" said Monro, and he went inside.

CHAPTER 29

I let myself into Pankhurst. The boarding house was never left empty during term time. I could hear the television in the junior common room.

"Hi," I said as I pushed the door open. The Furball was asleep on the velvet sofa with her mouth open. Her breathing was more laboured than usual, her nose was red and sore at the sides, and there were a couple of screwed-up pieces of kitchen towel next to her on the sofa, and a mug of what looked like cold Lemsip.

She stirred and woke up. "Kate," she said groggily. "Has Clemmie's concert finished?" She stared at the TV – the jaunty title sequence for a house makeover programme was playing. She looked even worse now she'd woken up.

"Yes, but I came back early from the tea. I'm going upstairs. Are you OK?"

"I should be in bed, but there are staffing issues." She reached for one of the pieces of kitchen towel and attempted to find a dry section to blow her nose on.

"I'll see you later," I said and scarpered.

I looked into the dining hall. The shutters were down in the kitchen, so I checked the folded invoice behind the Pankhurst portrait. It was still there. I'd never been on my own in Pankhurst before, or as alone as this. It gave me a small, unexpected thrill, and it occurred to me that as Head Prefect I could change the sad atmosphere in Pankhurst. What better tribute to Clemmie could there be than smashing one of the open house challenges? I would break into the kitchen to find where Squirrel hid her hairnets and take a selfie, or search for the key to the filing cabinet in the office to look inside. If I succeeded, I'd be able to picture her both impressed and furious, rather than broken at the bottom of the cliffs.

The shutters were impenetrable. People had tried to prise them open before. I went outside to see if any of the windows had been left open. There was one, but it was far too small for any human to squeeze through.

Taking a photo of the inside of the filing cabinet in the office might be easier; it was just a matter of finding the key, and with nobody else around I could have a thorough look. I'd already noticed the office wasn't locked when I'd come in. That was unlike Calding. When I went inside

I could see why. It looked as if she'd left to go to the memorial concert in a hurry. She'd been in the middle of packing up her things. There were two cardboard boxes on the desk, partially filled with her personal possessions: a hairbrush, handcream, a black cardigan, pens, calculator, phone charger and science textbooks. She was leaving. That was good news.

The shredder bin was full. There were piles of plastic sleeves crammed with spreadsheets. I glanced at them. Budgets. I opened the drawers of her desk. Envelopes, post-its, a hole-punch, clumps of dust ... and in the bottom drawer two keys. The bigger one looked like a spare key for the office door, and the smaller looked exactly like a filing cabinet key. I ran across the room with it. It fitted perfectly. It turned, and I said, "Yay," out loud. It had been so easy. I wished there was someone with me to share the moment.

The rumour had always been the cabinet was full of snacks. It wasn't, and I supposed I'd expected that. Even if there had been any left from Wibbz's era, Calding would have chucked them out when she arrived. There were loads of cardboard folders in there. Student files, I guessed. I took a quick photo on my phone for proof that I'd smashed the challenge.

I wasn't going to miss the opportunity of looking in my file. I listened to check the Furball wasn't moving around, then went to the window to see if anyone from Pankhurst was about to come in through the front door. Off in the

255

distance, at the end of the road I saw a navy puffa jacket. Damn. Calding. I'd only have a few minutes to check out what was in my file. The Js were in the third drawer down. My folder was surprisingly thick. As I pulled it out hastily, the flap tore a little, but I didn't let that worry me. I took the folder over to the desk and pushed the cardboard boxes away to give some space, and pulled out the wodge of paper inside.

There didn't seem to be any chronological order to the paperwork. The first page was a photocopy of vaccinations I'd had last year. I plucked out the original form my father had filled in after I'd been given a place at Pankhurst from somewhere near the middle. And ... what the hell ... reams of information about my plastic surgeries: printed-out email correspondence about what was then relatively recent plastic surgery, and follow-up appointments I needed to attend. There were photos of me before and after for reference, and notes about how I shouldn't play any contact sports for a while. There was an article about my father, torn from a newspaper, and photos of my parents in celebrity gossip magazines.

My heart was thudding. *Put the folder back*, I told myself. *Calding's on her way.* But I was confused. Who had added the extra things that definitely didn't need to be there? It came to me: Wibbz. She had been obsessed with our lives.

It clicked. This was where Clemmie must have found all her blackmail material. Somehow she'd had access to these files, and that maybe wasn't as hard as I thought when she was one of Wibbz's favourites and Wibbz was often drunk. Clemmie had smashed the open challenge long ago but hadn't told anyone because what she'd discovered was too valuable to let anyone else know.

I glanced out of the window. Calding was nearer but I still had another minute. I'd leave the office as soon as I heard her walk past. I went back to the files and selected Zeta's, keeping well away from the window so I couldn't be seen. I flicked through and saw there was information about her mother living abroad in a commune that didn't allow contact with the outside world. Someone had highlighted the name of the commune, and there were two articles about the commune, one a printed-out blogpost, and the other a more in-depth feature from an American newspaper.

I felt slightly sick. We were a kind of hobby for Wibbz, and Calding should have got rid of half this stuff.

I heard the brittle sound of shoes on the pavement outside. I had to leave. There was no time to look for anyone else's folder. I shoved the cabinet shut, and the key jammed as I turned it. I wrestled with it, yanking it out and running to the desk. I threw it into the drawer and ran out of the office and up the stairs as I heard Calding's key in the front-door lock. I'd made it out of sight just in time. I'd hide away upstairs and call Maria to see how Elsie Gran was doing.

Going along the second-floor landing and passing Clemmie's old bedroom, I thought of Ms Calding lurking nearby the evening I hid the delivery note. Had she been packing up Clemmie's stuff for her parents? I opened the door to peek in. It was bare, apart from the items every room possessed: bed, locker, chest of drawers, wardrobe and desk. The mattress had a quilted cover, which was creased and dented along one edge, as if someone had been sitting there. I didn't like being in that room. I almost had the feeling Clemmie might saunter in and catch me.

The door to my own bedroom was ajar. The cleaners had probably left it that way. That's what logic told me, but I was uneasy. As I touched the door to push it fully open, I knew in my core something was wrong.

My lungs flattened as I took in the devastation of my room. Someone had gone crazy in here. Everything had been swept on to the floor or smashed against the wall. Liquids and creams had been spilt on to my bedding, clothing had been ripped with scissors or destroyed with black marker pen, every drawer had been turned upside down, every photo ripped from the wall. My laptop screen was smashed and jewellery broken. This wasn't a burglary. This was a mad rage. I ran to Meribel's room. The contrast with my own was stark. Hers was exactly as she'd left it when she'd gone away. I moved on to Lo's room. It was orderly and perfect too. My heart beat faster and faster, and my mind swirled. Had somebody been looking for something? Was this about the delivery note? Or did someone do this because they hated me?

I was too shocked to cry yet and I couldn't face my own room again. I took my phone from my skirt pocket, and the piece of paper with Veronica's landline on it. I tapped in the number carefully, with shaking fingers, and sat on the top stair once it was ringing. It went to an answer service on the fourth ring. "Hello," I said. "This is a message for Veronica. It's Kate Jordan-Ferreira from Mount Norton. Please can you phone me back when you get a chance." I left my number and rang off.

I still had the number in my phone of the online pharmacy. If a different person answered, I'd ask again. I'd ask better.

"I wonder if you can help," I said after pressing four for "a problem with my order" and a man with an energetic voice had answered. "I'm a house mistress at a boarding school, and I have a problem which is rather delicate." I did my best to sound both authoritative and slightly gossipy.

"Oh yes?" said the man.

"Some girls have done a very silly prank with some stick-on sweat pads bought from your website."

The man at the other end of the phone made an "mmm" sound.

"I'm trying to deal with this in a sensitive manner without letting the whole boarding house know, so I'm contacting you to see who ordered them, so we can replace them. If I tell you the delivery address, would you be able to give me a name?"

"Do you have the order number? Or the date the item was ordered?"

"Oh. No. I'm afraid not."

"Let's see," said the man. "Give me the address, and the item."

I spelled out everything, aware of the noises in the house. A pipe was making a banging sound, and there was a faint scratching coming from nearby. I shuddered to think it could be a mouse or a rat. I waited.

"Right. Pankhurst House, you said? Got it."

Boom. I scrunched up in the pause, and stayed motionless. Was the man having second thoughts about telling me?

Don't say anything.

"Right. Just refreshing the page. Here it is ... three packs of our regular sweat pads were ordered by a Ms Scarlet Mires."

Scarlet Mires.

"*Scarlet* Mires, not Sasha Mires?" I queried slowly.

"Yes, Scarlet," said the man. His voice sounded far away.

Calding's first name was Scarlet. I grappled to understand what this meant.

"If you or Scarlet want to reorder the sweat pads, we've got a three-for-two offer on at the moment provided you—"

"Thank you," I interjected weakly. "Really helpful." I couldn't keep up the pretence of it any more, and I hung up.

Veronica must have picked the delivery note out of the recycling bin in the hall. Maybe she thought it was an old order, and that Sasha's real name was Scarlet. Veronica would have cut off the top of the paper to make it anonymous, and pretty much forgotten about it. Perhaps she saw Calding's first name in the newspaper and made the connection.

At the beginning of term, Tessa had said Calding had reminded her of someone.

Calding reminded her of Sasha.

Were Calding and Sasha related?

The house made another of its creaking sounds. It sounded as if there was someone on the stairs. I looked up. There was.

Calding.

CHAPTER 30

I stood up immediately. Fear flashed through me, instant and burning.

"Hello," she said. "That was an interesting phone call." Her face was greyish and unhealthy-looking, and one of her eyes was bloodshot.

She was blocking the stairs, so I went backwards towards my room. She stepped up on to the third-floor landing, one hand on the bannister.

"You're Scarlet Mires," I said. It sounded silly, but I knew it was true when I saw her face twitch.

"Scarlet Calding Mires," she said. "So much trouble over a delivery note which should have been shredded. One silly little slip-up." She shook her head. "I've disappointed myself." She clenched her free hand into a fist and hit her forehead with it. It shocked me. It must have hurt.

I couldn't remember the Furball's name for a moment. "Mrs Parwood?" I shouted, then more desperately "Mrs Parwood!"

"She won't hear you," hissed Calding.

There was no sound from downstairs. The implications of the empty house sunk in. I tensed my leg muscles to see if that would stop them shaking but it didn't. I had to keep her talking. I would distract her until I could shut myself in my bedroom and phone for help. If Calding was back, soon most of Pankhurst would be too.

"Are you Sasha's sister?" I asked. I could see it now. They did share similarities. They both had slim, athletic bodies and the same shape chins. I had a vague recollection that Sasha had a much older sister.

Calding said, "Half-sister, to be precise. You know, I used to think she was so lucky being able to come to this school. I didn't have this opportunity. But this school is cruel. Sasha was thrown out for something she didn't do, and nobody cared."

Sasha must have told her family about Wibbz's drinking. Had Calding been looking for an opportunity, a way in to get revenge?

I turned to make a dash for my room, but I'd forgotten there was so much broken stuff on the floor. I was too slow to get in and close the door before Calding reached it, and too caught up in pushing her out to see that she was after my phone.

"This needs to be confiscated," she said, holding it up. Her foot was against the door. I wasn't going to be able to keep her out.

I pointed to the wreckage of my room. "Did you do this?" I asked in a shaky voice, keeping my distance from her.

"I was angry," she said. "Very angry about my sister. You know, I was never jealous when my mum married my stepdad and they had Sasha. Never. All I ever wanted was a nice family with a dad and a sister." She stepped slowly over a mound of mutilated clothes. I moved towards the window: I'd run down the fire escape and go out of the back gate.

There was a crunching under my shoes, and I glanced down to see the remains of my Italian shot glasses.

"Sasha took her expulsion badly," said Calding. "We tried to help her, but she spiralled. Have you ever seen anyone lose hope? It's the worst thing. She was on medication that didn't suit her. The dosage was all wrong. We were trying to sort it out. Nobody cared. And then she walked right into traffic."

"I'm sorry," I said shakily.

"I'm the one who cares the most," said Calding. "Dad wrote letters, but what good do letters do?"

"Why did you take this job?" I whispered, even though I knew the answer.

She looked at me as if it was obvious. "To find out what happened. And I did. Clemmie told me everything that night, when she was on the edge of the cliff. She'd got away with too much. She didn't even touch the light switch. It wasn't fair. She needed to be punished."

The light switch? The one that shocked Paige?

So Calding had sabotaged it. I had a vision of her efficiently unscrewing the panel in her crisp white shirt.

"It seems you had quite a role in my sister's expulsion, didn't you?" said Calding.

"You killed Clemmie," I murmured. I couldn't control my breathing. It was making me dizzy. "You pushed her."

Calding nodded. "Lo kindly sent Sasha a text about your beach party. You less kindly told her not to come. I was going to shut it down, until I saw Clemmie on the path. I caught her by surprise as she was trying to take a photo. Such a vain girl – like you. And so selfish."

She bent to pick up something and the object in her hand glinted in the afternoon sunlight. A piece of glass. Her eyes were entirely focused on me now, and I turned to fumble with the window to the fire escape. It opened with a shudder and I stepped out. She grabbed my leg and I fell on to the metal. I had to get up. If I didn't get up. . .

"You're a fake, Miss Jordan-Ferreira," she said. "And you need to be punished too for what you did to my sister."

The image of the printout on Veronica's artwork flashed into my mind. It was her who'd put it up there.

She must have attached the printout of the hospital too. Was she behind the smashed sculpture and the graffiti as well?

"I'm so sorry," I cried. "You've already done enough," I pleaded, as I pulled away.

Her grip on my leg tightened, and her hand came near my face. It was bleeding from the glass. She hadn't noticed. She was too intent on reaching for me, almost rigid with determination. She was going to cut my face. I kicked out with my other leg and propelled myself along the metal fire escape platform, out of reach. My body was floppy with relief for an instant, but I had to move. Calding was climbing through the window.

I clattered down the fire escape. Through the haze of panic, I was aware of my own screams. I saw someone walking down the lane behind Pankhurst, and I screamed louder. They'd call the police. Soon there would be sirens. The man showed no sign of having heard me though – he carried on walking at the same pace. As I gave him a last yell, I saw he was wearing headphones.

There had to be someone in Churchill. Someone would hear me, but perhaps the housemaster I'd seen earlier had been the only person left and he was taking Monro to the police station.

If I ran to the gate I'd lose vital seconds inputting the code. Calding was behind me, not even out of breath. It was safer to run back into the house and out of the front door. I'd scream at the Furball to call the police.

I burst through the back door and the house vibrated with my voice. As I raced down the hallway to the junior common room, I pushed the door so hard it hit the wall with a bang, and bounced back, almost knocking me out.

What? In a split second I could see the room was empty. The Furball had gone. The screwed-up pieces of kitchen towel and the mug of Lemsip were no longer there. I was dimly aware the makeover show had got to the reveal stage.

"I sent Mrs Parwood home," said Calding, immediately behind me. She shoved me into the junior common room. The intensity of her eyes was chilling. "She wasn't well."

"Where's everyone else?" I wished I hadn't asked out loud.

"They won't be back for ages," said Calding.

I thought of Zeta, wanting to slip away from the tea. She'd be back any minute.

"Everyone had to return to their last lesson of the day after the tea. Did you miss that announcement because you'd sneaked out with your boyfriend? We've got plenty of time before we're disturbed. I've only got a few things I need to do before I leave here for good. Boarding school life isn't for me." She advanced with her piece of glass.

I looked around wildly for something to protect myself with. All I could reach was a cushion. Calding was backing me into the corner of the room. I knew the windows would be locked. They didn't open this end because they faced on to the road. I was going to be sliced with that piece of glass in Calding's hand. I gagged at the memory of Clemmie's body on the rocks, the blood still leaving it.

The sound of the front door opening surprised us both. Zeta!

Calding was quicker to react than me. She lunged at me, grabbed the cushion, and held it against my face. I struggled to breathe. Panic flooded my veins.

"In here," shouted Calding. "The junior common room." She released the cushion slightly and held the glass against my throat. As it touched my skin, I froze. "Keep quiet," she whispered.

The footsteps came nearer, sure and certain on the polished tiled floor. The presenter on the TV programme was saying goodbye. I held my breath. If I breathed in too far, would that exert too much pressure against the glass? Calding had her eyes on the door.

It swung open. "Ms Calding, I was told you wanted to see m—" It wasn't Zeta. It was Lo. She stepped back, her face rigid with the shock of seeing Calding's bloody hands at my throat.

Our eyes met. I saw the horror of my situation reflected in them.

"Ah, perfect. Hand over your phone," said Calding. "Or I slice Kate's throat."

With trembling hands, Lo swung her backpack round and unzipped the front pocket for her phone.

"Hurry up," snapped Calding. She moved the glass

away from my neck but kept a tight hold of my arm. "Put it on the mantelpiece where I can see it."

Lo did as she was told. "What's going on?" she croaked.

"As your friend here – ex-friend – recently discovered, I'm Sasha's half-sister," said Calding.

Lo swallowed and exchanged a horrified look with me.

"I'm so glad you could join us, Lois. You knew my sister the best and still you took everyone else's side. You didn't believe that she might be innocent, did you?"

Lo swallowed. She was choosing her words carefully. "Not straightaway. I'm really sorry. We went to the hospital to hand her a card."

I was grateful Lo included me in the last sentence.

Calding snapped, "I know. Too little too late."

Lo suddenly ran at Calding, going for her hand with the piece of glass. Calding dropped the glass, but swung her arm back and punched Lo in the head. The single blow felled her. I screamed and shot across the room for the phone on the mantelpiece. Holding it was the last thing I remembered before everything went black.

The first thing I noticed when I opened my eyes was the insistent siren-like noise, which seemed to pulse in time with my aching head. Next, I became aware of the smell. Smoke. I felt strangely calm until I turned my head and saw flames leaping above the grey-black smoke pouring off the curtains and the sofa. I sat up and coughed.

"Lo?" She was lying exactly how she'd fallen when Calding hit her. There was no reply.

The room was becoming darker from the smoke. We didn't have long to get out of here. I'd watched a video once about staying low to the ground to avoid smoke. The door to the junior common room was closed. I crawled over to try the handle. The metal burned my hands. I pulled my school jumper over one hand and tried again. It was locked.

We were trapped. I couldn't breathe.

The tears on my cheeks were too hot. In a minute, I was going to choke. I would drown in this smoke. I couldn't see further than a metre or so in front of me.

The windows were old. They were locked, but old. They'd smash. Please God, they'd smash. But I needed to find Lo first.

I felt the ground in front of me. The rug was already hot. The fireplace wasn't ever used but there were fireside tools in a revolving set. They might be too hot to touch by now, but I was near the fireplace. I could feel the stone hearth. There. I had a poker in my hand, and it hurt so much to hold it. I smashed it against the fireplace to wake Lo up. And again. I hit the fireplace with all my strength until I realized how stupid I was to sap my strength like that.

I crawled forward, fumbling for Lo's body. I must have been disorientated, heading round in circles, and then I felt her soft, motionless body.

270

I dragged her past the armchair and the coffee table. I kept squeezing her arm, hoping she'd wake. Eventually, we reached the end of the room and I felt my way up to the window. I lifted the neck of my jumper over my nose to help me breathe. I was suffocating. I coughed so much I was sick. I wasn't sure where my sick had landed but I could smell it mixed in with the smoke. My eyes and nose streamed. The smoke alarm seemed more distant now.

I had to be sure I was ready to strike the window because standing up would be unbearable for too long. Gripping the poker, I counted down in my head.

I slammed the poker against the glass. The noise was hopeful but the glass didn't budge, even when I shoved my shoulder against it. I ducked down to breathe. I let my head flop back. This was futile. I dropped the poker and lay down, feeling for Lo's hand. I squeezed it. She'd been such a good friend in this place, and I'd let her down, just as much as I'd let Sasha down.

Coughing. I couldn't stop.

I was Kate Lynette Jordan-Ferreira.

I was fearless.

I would do this.

I would die doing this.

Grab that heavy poker. Rise up. Kneel. Cough. On my feet. Cough. Hit the glass. *Crack. Crack. Crack.* The smoke appeared to move like a snake through the small opening.

Crack. Crack. Voices. Someone yelled, "There are girls in here."

Everything shattered. It was raining glass, and I lay down to shield Lo, and I gulped and coughed and retched. I could do this. I lifted Lo, flopped her against my shoulder, and heaved her up. I knew what a fireman's lift was. I knew more useful stuff than I thought I did. Strong hands helped me get Lo through the window, and then it was my turn. I climbed out, and someone clapped my shoulder, and blackness from my clothes, skin and hair puffed into the air, and it still hurt to breathe, and I was about to be sick again, but I could smell the sea, and I heard someone say, "Tell Monro she's safe."

THE BEACH

Monro and I walk along the beach together. It's sunset, and we aren't going to get back to our boarding houses before curfew. We might end up grounded for a few days, but it'll be worth it. It's a special evening: the sky's bright pink and purple, the air is warm, the beach is empty, and it's my birthday.

Pankhurst was refurbished, but I haven't gone inside the building again. After I was discharged from hospital, I returned to Elsie Gran's. My parents flew over to see me for a couple of days and there were discussions about which school I was going to when I was well enough.

I finally got my own way: I'm back at Mount Norton, but I'm at a different boarding-house.

I'll finish out the year and do my exams. Changing schools in the fifth form wasn't going to do anything for my grades. Ms Calding ruined so much, and I'm not going to let her set back my future. I realized I'm competitive. I like to do well.

For sixth form, I'm going to a college local to Elsie Gran. I've looked round it and it's going to suit me fine. I already know Josie, and she says I can hang with her and her crew.

Lo never came back at all. She couldn't face it. She was given a scholarship transfer to another school. Meribel dropped out to do more modelling, and is allegedly being home schooled. I'm in touch with both of them, and I miss them.

I have a room next door to Zeta in my new boarding house. She moved over after the fire. I'm getting to know her, and she's not quite as feeble as I thought she was, but that freaky hamster cushion is not allowed anywhere near me.

There's currently no House Prefect at Pankhurst, but a new one will be appointed next term. I heard there'll be a proper vote.

I haven't seen Veronica since the beach house party. Monro says she goes to a day school near where they both live, and when I visit his family in the summer, we can meet up. The summer is still a way away, and I like that he thinks we'll still be together then.

People talk about what happened with Calding from

time to time. They say they knew there was something psychopathic about her all along, and I think, "Sure. It's easy to say that now." There's a trial coming up, and Lo and I have to be there. It won't be pleasant, but I've learned it's better if you face up to stuff.

Sasha is in the process of recovering. One day soon, Lo and I are going to visit her. We want to see her before the trial starts. I want to apologize in person.

Kipper's disappeared. The café was closed down for a bit until a couple took over. They do organic fruit smoothies and vegan all-day breakfasts now. Parents have started going there, which is annoying.

We have a new headmistress. Ms Sneller was asked to leave by the governors. There were things she handled badly, including not properly investigating what happened between Bernard and me. I told Elsie Gran about Bernard when she drove me back to Mount Norton. I asked her to turn off the audiobook and listen, and not say anything.

She had plenty to say of course, but she mostly said it to the school. The police were involved, and Bernard ended up moving schools. I was told his new school is aware of his record in case anything else happens. I hope he's faced up to what he did.

Monro stumbles on a pebble and I grip his hand tightly, and we both stay upright. He's on new drugs, and the stumbles hardly ever happen any more.

"Nice try," I say. "You nearly had me on the ground then. Pick a more comfortable landing next time."

He laughs, and double squeezes my hand, then lets go and runs towards the water's edge. He prances around the edge of the water, playing a game of chicken with the tiny waves. I take photos of him. I'll time-lapse it later. At the end of this term, after my exams, I'll be leaving, and I want to have some of these escapades with Monro recorded. To remember the happy times.

I pull him away before the inevitable happens. I don't want him moaning about soggy feet and ruined trainers. We cuddle up for the walk past the spot where Clemmie's body was found. There are flowers on the rocks, as there are from time to time, placed there by Paige and the rest of their crowd. The week I came back to Mount Norton, I placed some there myself. I was going to add a note, but I didn't in the end. What I wanted to say was too complicated, and too private. I knew other people would read it, like I read other people's notes. We would always have been enemies, me and Clemmie, but it was shocking to think that she'd never experience the rest of her life.

"I like how the flowers dry out and the wind scatters them," I say to Monro when we're past the site.

"It's not like she'll be forgotten," says Monro. "There's the stained-glass window, for starters."

I can't help giggling, and Monro raises his eyes at me, "Is that an appropriate response to a serious memorial, Miss Kate Jordan-Ferreira?" The stained glass window in the assembly hall is monstrous in size and design, depicting with various green geometric shapes the countryside where Clemmie was apparently happiest. An amazing amount of money has been raised in Clemmie's name, a lot of it funded quietly by the school according to Squirrel, who's now got a job in the main school kitchen. The best memorial is the Clementine Hillard scholarship, which was awarded to Zeta so she can stay on into the sixth form. I love the sweet irony of that.

We carry on, past the area of blackened stones where Hugo had a barbecue a couple of nights ago for the Churchill party. We heard it wasn't a success. Local residents complained to the police, and it got shut down before it had got properly going. Monro and I didn't go. Fire scares me now, and I'm so done with boosting Hugo's ego.

"Don't make me run up the steps," says Monro. "I don't want anything to happen to my bag."

I don't know what is in there for sure, but I know he was on the coach to Ryemouth the day before yesterday, and I decide to play safe. At the top, we turn right. I glance back at the beach house, glad we aren't going to walk past it. It looks dark, presumably unoccupied.

"Come on," says Monro, tugging my hand. "Onwards to the horrible, rotting bench."

"You know the best places," I say. I'm actually not joking. The bench has become one of our favourite spots. There is a mound of weed-covered earth behind it, and if we place Monro's old grey rug on it and use the back of the bench as a footrest, there is a fantastic view of the sea and the Isle of Wight. We sometimes somersault backwards into the soft landing of the bracken behind it.

Monro lays out a squashed chocolate fudge cake from the bakery in Ryemouth, proper plates and a knife pinched from Churchill dining hall, and some napkins snaffled from Pret A Manger.

"Before you say anything, these have LED batteries," says Monro, bringing out a few tea lights. He switches them on at the base, and they give out a yellow glow from their fake flame. After more rummaging some miniature bottles of rum appear, then a can of Coke and some plastic glasses. "Or if you prefer," says Monro, "Voila!" He pulls out his thermos with a flourish, as if it's a bottle of champagne.

He says I have to eat some cake before I open his present, which is a tiny package wrapped in navy blue tissue paper and tied with a silver ribbon bow.

"Why?" I ask.

"So you still feel happy in case you don't like what I've bought you."

I smile. Whatever he's bought will be perfect because he was thinking of me at the time. I slice the cake, eat a huge mouthful, and then undo the bow. There's a box beneath the tissue paper, and nestled inside is a silver necklace with a bright blue crystal attached. "It represents trust and faith," he says, laughing awkwardly. "I mean, who knows if that's really true. It's what the woman in the shop told me, and I thought you'd like the colour, and the

278

trust/faith thing is kind of appropriate with you leaving Mount Norton in June..." He's gone red.

I nod and hold the necklace up, thanking him. Even in this dimming light, it reflects and shines back many variations of blue. "It's beautiful," I say. I open the clasp and put it on. "Look!" I say, and stand up on the bench to pose. The rotten wood shifts suddenly and I squeal and launch myself back on the earth pile, and Monro catches me, and draws me close. I touch his face with my burn-scarred hands. My face is still beautiful and I'm grateful. There's no shame in that.

We lean in to kiss.

ACKNOWLEDGEMENTS

Over the course of writing this book I learned a lot about kindness, something which is in short supply at my fictional boarding school. My biggest thanks go to the Nossiter family, especially Fiona, David and my goddaughter Morgan. Also to the Johnson family, especially Jen, Adam and Billy. So many people have helped me far more than they realise, including Laura Steinberger, Andrew Goodwillie, Cath Howe, Juliet Hartridge, and the Munster Road Mafia, and I hope I can pay it forward.

Thanks, as always, to my agent Becky Bagnell for being so helpful, and to my editors Linas Alsenas and Eishar Brar for helping to shape this story. Thank you to Liam Drane for a clever cover design, Pete Matthews for razor-sharp copy-editing, Harriet Dunlea for publicity, and the rest of the hard-working team at Scholastic UK.

Thank you to Ashley Postans for answering my dodgy questions about electric shocks.

A big hello to Esher High School students (especially the fabulous library monitors), my Hub colleagues Mrs Smith and Mrs Fairey, the homework club crew Ms McCartney and Mrs Dallamore and the Inclusion Support Base squad Mrs Power, Miss Emerton and Mr Highman (not forgetting Teddy, everyone's favourite cavapoo).

Heartfelt hugs to my family: Mum, Dad, Clare, Dave, James, Tom, Nick, Esther, Niamh, Phoebe, Maia and Sophie.

Finally, thank you to everyone who has championed my books, and encouraged me along the writing path. I have very much appreciated it.